ROUGH AND READY

MORE THAN A COWBOY - 2

VANESSA VALE

D1517602

GET A FREE VANESSA VALE BOOK!

Join Vanessa's mailing list to be the first to know of new releases, free books, special prices and other author giveaways.

http://freeromanceread.com

1

ℋARPER

"You owe me," Cam snapped.

Hearing my brother's voice made me shudder. Bile rose in my throat. He'd started calling me two weeks ago, prompting me to his release date. I hadn't needed any reminder. The date was etched in my brain, and every time I looked at the calendar, I saw it creep closer.

Owe him? Owe him money for what he did? My hand shook as I held my cell to my ear. It didn't surprise me that he'd found me. Again. Even after a new cell number. I was stupid to think that would have worked to keep him away.

"For what?" I asked, my voice shrill. I tried to sound calm because he thrived on making me upset. He'd use it, prey on it, just like he was preying on me, even from behind bars.

"All that money you have is because of me."

I paced to the windows that overlooked the busy street. I'd just moved into the apartment, so there were only basic white blinds for privacy, but I kept them up to let in the weak December sunshine. With darkness falling fast and knowing Cam was out there, even in jail, I tugged at the cord, pulled one down. Then the next and next down the length of the wall until I couldn't see out, until I was in my little cocoon where nothing could get me. Yeah, right. I wrapped my arm about my waist, suddenly cold. Alone.

"You gave me to two thugs in trade for erasing your gambling debts," I countered, running a hand over my face, through my hair. I'd pulled it back this morning into a reasonably artful twist for work, but with one swipe of my palm, I'd messed it all up.

I didn't want to rehash what he'd done because he was well aware of it, but he didn't think it mattered. Antsy, I spun on my heel and went to an open moving box sitting on my desk. A plant was stacked haphazardly on top of a bunch of office supplies, and I set it down with a hard thunk on the bare surface. It needed water after sitting neglected for over a week.

"Yeah, and nothing happened to you except getting a fuck-ton of Mommy and Daddy's cash."

Nothing happened? I pulled the phone away from my ear and stared at it. My palms were sweating, and a dull ache took up residence at the back of my head.

"They attacked me in an elevator."

"They didn't *rape* you or anything."

Rape was his baseline for whether something *happened,* and that made me sick. Everything about Cameron made me sick. As my older brother, he was supposed to be my protector, watching out for things like handsy boyfriends. He'd been a little shit since maybe the terrible twos and never grew out of it. We'd never once played together as kids, hadn't even gone to the same prep school. We'd never bonded over video games or hours of sitting in the back seat on a road trip.

Instead, he considered me as more of a *thing*. A thing he'd given to two men. I'd escaped them physically unharmed, but they'd never been caught. The case was still open, and they were still out there. My brother wouldn't reveal their names, knowing he'd be dead if he snitched. I should've had Cam arrested, too, for his involvement, but no.

My parents had only thought of Cam and their reputation—which only enabled his drug-fueled habits. They'd forced me to keep quiet about his whole "sisterly sell-off," and I had a huge stash of hush money in the bank as extra incentive to prove it.

I'd been too traumatized at the time to fight them. I *would* have given Cam up to the police once I stopped having constant nightmares and wasn't too afraid to go outside, but he'd been dumb enough to be caught a few weeks later as a first time drug offender and went to jail anyway. All on his own. Nothing dear old Mom and Dad could do about that one.

"Leave me alone," I said, my voice flat.

His upcoming release was the reason I'd moved. Again. He'd known where I'd lived, and with him getting out, I hadn't felt safe. Soon enough, he'd be able to show up with anyone. Anytime.

No, this place was safer than my old house closer to campus. I looked around. A modern, high-end building. Three floors, only three apartments with tight security. Not only did my landlord, Grayson Green—one of the most famous and successful MMA fighters—live on the top floor, but another guy who he trained had the unit across from mine on the second. On the ground floor, a whole gym full of guys who wouldn't hesitate to even the score for me. At least that was what my friend, Emory, had told me. I'd lived on the same block as her before she moved in with Gray, her fiancé.

"Leave you alone? Wire me the money, and I will," Cam snapped. "And Harper—"

"Fuck you." I ended the call, tossed my phone on the couch, not wanting to hear anything else from him. He'd spent almost two years preparing to destroy me again. Now that his release day was close, I knew the phone calls were just the start. Even after switching numbers, he still found me.

I paced the room, back and forth, weaving around boxes and randomly placed furniture where the movers had set it down. The apartment had an open floor plan, one big room except for the powder room, bedroom and master bath. The ceilings were high, the windows big and wall-to-wall. It was modern with lots of stainless-steel appliances in the kitchen, but it was warm. Safe.

I'd moved in a week ago and hadn't settled. I'd only put my bed together, tossed my clothes into the bedroom and found the coffeemaker. Hell, based on the damn call, I had to wonder how long I could remain. I'd easily avoided my parents since the *incident,* but we didn't run in the same social scene. I didn't spend time in the country club circle. I was too academic, too pedantic in my field of study for them. Instead of being a lawyer, I'd balked at the whole Lane family tradition and became a professor. To them, even with my PhD, it was a very small step up from working retail.

When Cam got out, would he be banging on my door harassing me? Or worse, on the street? On the quad at school? Could I stay in Brant Valley? Instead of settling into this great apartment, I wondered how long I'd be able to live in town. Hell, the state.

The call was all part of Cam's plan to fuck with me. A warm up. I knew it, but I couldn't help but freak out.

The plant was in my hand and beneath the sink faucet before I realized what I was doing. I didn't even remember grabbing it or walking into the kitchen. I closed my eyes, breathed.

I didn't want *Mommy and Daddy's* cash. I didn't want my parents in my life any more than my brother, so I'd shoved the money in the bank where no one could touch it. My parents couldn't get it back, and Cam couldn't reach it.

They'd picked their son, with his cruel and dangerous acts, over their own daughter. And their money? I'd give it all away just to get Cam out of my life permanently, but I wouldn't give in. I wouldn't give him the hush money. And it *was* hush money.

No one could know that Cameron Lane the Third had an addiction problem who'd traded his own sister to drug dealers in exchange for wiping his debt clean. That kind of thing didn't happen at the country club, and it certainly didn't happen to my parents.

But it had happened to *me*.

Realizing I was drowning the plant, I turned off the water and pushed back from the sink. Closed my eyes and groaned aloud. My frustration was coming off me in waves. I was beyond climbing in bed and throwing the covers over my head. Beyond tears. There just weren't any more left. I'd stopped crying two years ago.

Going into the bedroom, I kicked off my heels, stripped off my skirt and blouse and dug out my gym clothes from the pile in the corner. I usually waited until later in the evening to work out, coming home from work and eating first, but I had restless energy to burn. I needed to run this angst off. I'd taken up running after the *incident*, my therapist said exercise was like a release valve on a pressure cooker.

I hadn't liked being compared to a kitchen appliance, but I related. I had been ready to blow, and running had helped. I hadn't made it far at first, walking more than anything else, but now, now I could run for hours, especially when I was upset. After slipping a hair tie around my wrist, I found my running shoes by the door, sat down on the wood floor, tugged one on, worked the laces with extra vigor.

I was safe. I knew it. Cameron was still in jail. The men who'd attacked me would have come after me again way before now if they'd still wanted me. The way I figured it, and the police assumed as well, was that they wanted Cam. If that were true, they could have him. I could only imagine how much he'd liked to be assaulted by them.

My apartment was safe. Gray had reassured me personally. Key cards were required for the elevator and emergency stairs, and only the four residents had them. Gray liked things secure. While he knew how to fight, and fight well, he only liked using his fists in the ring. Those were his words when he'd handed me my key card, which had been reassuring. Besides, he wouldn't have risked Emory's safety for anything. I'd lived down the street from her, where we'd been neighbors for the three years while I was teaching classes and finishing my dissertation for my PhD. After the incident, I hadn't ever really felt safe. Emory had thought of me for the vacant unit, and she'd assured me it was secure.

I was safe.

That didn't mean I wasn't riled, wouldn't have nightmares about what happened on the elevator. Again.

Cameron's few calls always brought them back. The anxiety always returned. Like now, when I wanted to run until my legs gave out, until, hopefully, I was too exhausted to even dream.

Finished with my shoes, I stood, grabbed my car keys, the building key pass and went to one of the piles of boxes. A few had to go to my office for my next semester Medieval Art class, so I'd use my angst to lug them to my car for tomorrow. I stacked three identical ones, heavy with books, on the moving dolly. Pulling the cart behind me, I went out into the hall, locked my apartment. Looked longingly at the stairwell door. I hated elevators. After what happened, it had taken six months just to ride in one again. Now, I'd take them, but only with others, those I trusted. Or in safe places. Like one I shared with only three other people.

There was no way I'd get down the stairs with the boxes, and I wasn't making three trips. Pulling the dolly in behind me, I took a deep breath, pressed the button for the ground floor.

Still, I dreaded stepping inside when the door slid open. I thought of the two men who'd been on either side of me, one turning to press me into the wall, his hands groping. The other had watched, laughed.

I pushed the memories away, stepped inside, pushed the button for the ground floor. Willed the sick feeling down. I needed to chill. To unwind. To forget about Cam. What he'd done. What he wanted now. I'd burn off my anger on the treadmill in Gray's gym since it got dark so early. I wasn't running by myself outside at night. Not this time of year.

Exercise always worked. I could do this, I could get over Cam's call, the greasy thoughts of those men, how one had held me as the other ripped my shirt. How I'd kicked and fought, broke a nose. The blood. The panic. The debilitating need to have the doors open to escape. The stumble onto the marble floor in front of the bank of elevators. The cry for security.

I remembered the feel of their rough hands. Heard their voices telling me what they were going to do to me. Smelled their cloying cologne, the cheap cigarettes.

The elevator doors slid open. I took one step, and my breath caught in my lungs when I saw him.

Him.

Big. Broad. Tattooed. Thickly muscled. Chiseled jaw. Angry eyes. A palpable energy radiated from him. He looked mean. Bad. Ruthless. His hands were clenched in fists, and he stepped toward me, then froze when he saw me. His look changed then, the fury slipping away.

Still, he scared the shit out of me. For a split second, I thought he was going to hurt me.

No. This guy wasn't planning on dragging me to a hotel room and raping me. He was... trying to go upstairs. I *knew* this. My brain processed that he lived in the building or at least had a key card to call the elevator. But no. That didn't matter. *Run! Run!* were my only thoughts.

No. I couldn't look like a complete lunatic, couldn't let my fear rule me. I let out a deep breath and murmured, "Excuse me."

He stepped back, hands raised in front of his chest, and I pulled the dolly with the boxes into the lobby area.

I heard the elevator close, felt the keen sense of panic start to wane. I stopped just inside the exterior doors, stared outside through the glass. At nothing. Breathed. Tried to calm my racing heart. Cam had done this to me. Made me a quivering mess, scared of everything. Even my neighbor.

Of course, the intense man was my neighbor. I'd met Gray and Emory. They told me Gray's fighter, Reed, lived in the other apartment on my floor, but I hadn't met him yet. I'd been in the gym twice so far—Gray offered membership with the rent—and seen a number of fighters working out in the ring as I ran on the treadmill but didn't know which one was him. The number of fit guys, punching, kicking and rolling around on the ground trying to choke each other was enough to make any woman's ovaries perk up and take notice. I had no idea sweaty men could be so arousing.

But none of them had anything on Reed. Even through my panic, I was attracted. Perhaps that was why I *was* so panicked. In that split second, I shouldn't have desired the man who could do me harm. If I took away the layers of panic, I'd remember his height, at least a half a foot taller than me. Jet black hair had been cut super short, as if he used clippers himself instead of going to a barber. His skin was olive toned, and the start of a beard made his square jaw rugged.

Then there were the tattoos. Swirls of color and shapes crept up his arms, and I had no doubt more were hidden beneath his shirt. The overall effect screamed bad boy.

His dark eyes had widened in surprise at the sight of me, then a touch more after that, probably because I'd stared at him in horror. With his nose that had a crook in it and the splotchy red marks on his left cheekbone, he looked like he'd been in old fights and new ones. A snug white t-shirt had been plastered to his skin with sweat, the collar slightly stretched as if yanked a few times, and a pair of black workout shorts rode low on his hips. He was a fighter not a rapist.

I pushed open the outer door with more aggression than needed and tugged on the dolly, wheeling it to the back of my car. No doubt Reed thought I was insane. At the least, deathly afraid of him. My heart still hammered. My throat burned with the need to cry, but there were no tears. Cam had done this to me. Even after two years, even from a jail cell, he held so much power over me. He was still fucking with me. My work, my life, my relationships. When he got out...

As I stuffed the boxes in the trunk of my car, I had to wonder if I'd ever be free. And a guy like Reed? I wasn't a damsel in distress worth saving.

2

EED

I HAD no idea what the fuck happened with my new neighbor. I had women stop in their tracks and stare at me with a quick eagerness that said they'd get on their knees for me in the nearest bathroom. I'd never had a woman look at me with such horror. Yeah, I was dangerous, but not to women. Not to *her*.

I'd just finished up a few rounds with a kid who wanted to be an MMA fighter, so I was a little sweaty, a little pissed. He'd sworn he was the next big thing and wanted Gray, also known as The Outlaw—who was the best trainer around, perhaps one of the best fighters even after his retirement—to check him out. Gray had put him through his paces in the ring with me. He hadn't done it for the punk. Gray had known he wouldn't cut it because of his piss-poor attitude alone. He'd done it for Emory, his fiancée, who worked with the kid's dad at the hospital.

Gray wouldn't do shit like that for anyone else. Hell, he'd handed her his balls the day they met last summer, but he seemed just fine with it. Emory was killer, and I didn't say that about too many women, especially the groupies who only wanted to be taken for a ride on an MMA fighter's dick. They were good for a quick release, but that was it.

The kid was all attitude, no footwork, and I knew Gray wanted me to take him down a notch or two. I'd put him on the ground several times, which only pissed him off. He hadn't even landed a punch, not until after the bell, and he came after me. I was used to guys' egos, but this little fuck? Yeah, Gray wasn't going to work with him, and he'd have to deal with any fallout for Emory with the doctor. I didn't think there would be much because not many people crossed The Outlaw. And if I stood beside him? Yeah, the doc would piss himself.

I was angry about the sucker punch, so instead of hitting him right back—which was what I would have done a few years ago as a punk on the streets—I let Gray deal with him. I walked off, heading to my apartment to shower, to chill with a protein drink and some crappy TV. Not used to anyone being in the elevator—it had only been Gray and Emory who also lived above the gym until last week—I almost bumped into her. *Her.*

The look on her face stopped me cold better than a fist to the face from any fighter.

She hadn't been just startled or surprised. No, she'd been fucking petrified. I swore I saw all color drain from her face when she got a glimpse of me. Her eyes had widened, then darted past my shoulder at her only means of escape. A shiver had gone through her as if she'd been exorcised of a ghost. Then, all of a sudden, she pulled herself together and moved past me, fast, lugging a moving dolly loaded with boxes. I'd held my hands up and took a step back, letting her know without words I meant her no harm. It didn't matter. The damage had somehow been done.

I knew I was pretty scary looking. Being six-three, I loomed over people. I had shoulders like a linebacker and tattoos covered my arms. My nose was crooked, and my jaw was a little sore from where the kid sucker punched me.

I'd been told I looked fucking mean. A lot of the time, I *felt* mean. I was dark on the inside. Angry, dangerous. I wasn't the asshole I used to be. I wasn't the fucked-up kid. The army and training with Gray had set me straight. Still, grown men gave me plenty of room on the sidewalk. But this? With Harper—Emory had told me her name—this was different. I didn't like it at all. I didn't want someone like her to fear me.

I didn't get on the elevator. I couldn't just ignore the fact that I'd frightened her. I stood there, watched as she walked quickly toward the outside doors. Stopped. She didn't know I was watching her, perhaps thought I'd gone upstairs. She looked down at the ground, her body shaking. Shit. I'd done that to her. I wanted to go to her, grab her in my arms and let her know she was safer with me than anywhere else, but that wasn't going to work. Not now.

After a few seconds, she lifted her chin, rolled her shoulders back. I could see she was taking deep breaths, and her fingers relaxed around the handle of the dolly.

She was tall and dressed in a t-shirt and running shorts. I couldn't miss her slim shape. Her legs were long, well-muscled. Between the shapely calves and the running shoes, I guessed her workout choice. Was she going for a run now, once she ditched those boxes? While it wasn't even six, it was dark out. Cold, too. While this wasn't a dangerous part of town, it wasn't safe for her to run alone at night, anywhere. So I'd stick around and make sure she didn't do something stupid.

Yeah, that was the reason why I leaned against the wall, took stock of my new neighbor.

Her dark hair was sleek and stick straight, grazing her shoulders. It had to be silky soft to touch. When she'd freaked, I hadn't missed her dark eyes, the high cheekbones, full lips. As she stood there and pulled herself together, I took the time to notice her perfect ass and toned thighs.

I was a red-blooded male, and she was hot. I couldn't help but notice, couldn't help I had to adjust my dick in my workout shorts. While I liked a woman all feminine in dresses and heels, I also liked one who wasn't high maintenance. Who took care of herself. Saw fitness as healthy.

Pushing the outer door open, she went out into the parking lot. It was well lit—Gray was more of a freak about safety than anyone I knew—and using a key fob, she popped the trunk on a dark colored sedan. If she hadn't been afraid of me, I'd have gone out and helped because I didn't let a woman lug a bunch of boxes around, but if she lost it at the sight of me at the elevator, I didn't know what she'd do if I joined her in a parking lot at night. Did she have mace on that keychain?

I watched her put the three boxes away, close the trunk. She went into the gym through its main entrance, not through the side door off of the lobby. I went there and peeked in, watched as she set the dolly in the corner by the gym's coat rack, gave a shaky wave to Jack at the front desk, then made her way to the row of treadmills that looked out onto the street. Good girl.

My neighbor was skittish as fuck yet smart. She wasn't running outside.

After stepping on and pushing a few buttons, she started walking, tugging an elastic band from her wrist and pulling her hair back into a sloppy tail. Yeah, she wasn't high maintenance or trying to catch the eyes of the guys. While those shorts showed off a mile of leg, she was dressed fairly modestly. No tight yoga pants or snug top.

After pressing a few more buttons on the treadmill, her pace quickened. By the time I pushed through the door and leaned against the front desk, she was running at a serious pace. No warm up.

Gray's gym had free weights and exercise machines, treadmills and ellipticals, but he specialized in MMA fighting. This meant a large amount of real estate devoted to all aspects of mixed martial arts; an open mat, separate training rooms, and an octagon with a fence around it, just like the ones on TV. His members were those like Harper who needed a place to get a workout in who had no interest in fighting. Yoga and spin classes were on the schedule for them. Then there were the serious competitors like me. MMA, Muay Thai, BJJ and other fighting classes were filled with those who wanted to compete or at least defend themselves. Gray intentionally kept it from being a total meat market and a straight competition gym. The balance worked, and it was considered one of the best gyms in town.

"I thought you went to shower," Jack said, frowning at me. He was in college, working the desk in exchange for free membership. While he didn't have aspirations of being the next big fighter, he took all the classes Gray offered. His focus was BJJ, and he'd just gotten his blue belt. He had the physique for the sport, and the time on the mat with more experienced people kept his ego in check.

Manning the desk, he couldn't have missed what happened earlier in the ring with the doc's kid. Gray was in his glass enclosed office talking to the dickhead, who was wiping his sweaty head with one of the gym's white towels. While Gray was chill as he leaned back in his desk chair, the other guy was pissed and waving his arms. Probably spouting some shit about being a great fighter. Whatever.

I glanced back at my new neighbor. Her ponytail swung side to side as she ran. The treadmills faced the front windows. During the day, the street was visible and watching traffic helped pass the monotony of running nowhere. I hated running inside, but bad weather this time of year forced me on them sometimes as part of my workout. No way would I risk injury because of ice.

"Your new neighbor, right?" Jack asked. "She's pretty serious."

"Serious? You mean personality?" I asked. I picked up a pen, fiddled with it, tried not to show the depth of my interest in her. The last thing I needed was for Jack to think I was a seventh-grade girl interested in gossip.

"Nah, she's cool. Introduced herself the other day. She runs."

"Yeah, I can see that," I countered, watching her smooth pace, the way the muscles in her legs moved with each step.

"No, I mean she *runs*."

I turned to look at him. "What the fuck does that mean?"

He rolled his eyes. "It means she came in yesterday before the BJJ class. We talked about stupid shit for a few minutes before she went to the treadmills. Asked me about the classes I was taking. Did you know she's a professor at the university? Teaches some obscure art topic." He thought for a second. "I don't remember which." He leaned in. "I have to admit, she's really pretty, and I wasn't listening all that closely."

I grinned when I saw a flush climb up his cheeks. Yeah,

she was *pretty*. And then some. What guy could process words when a girl like her offered a soft smile? I'd gotten horror, and I was still intrigued.

"So, running?" I asked, getting him back on track. I didn't think it was a safe topic for him to talk about how hot one of the gym's members was, especially since he was on the clock. It was fine for me to *think* it, but I wasn't going to tell him that.

"She was running like she is now when Paul took over the desk, so I could go into class."

That meant fast. She wasn't jogging, not like Jimmy, one of the gym regulars, two treadmills over. He kept turning his head to watch her, even pushed some buttons on his machine to pick up his pace, clearly not interested in being outdone.

I knew he did three miles as part of his workout routine, and she made him look like he was hobbling along with a walker. With the faster speed, he was failing quickly, and I had to shake my head.

"She was still running at the same pace when I came out."

Whoa. I gave him a look, knowing Jack liked to stretch the truth. "Class was an hour."

Jack grabbed a membership card from a guy who came in, scanned it. Tossed him a towel.

"Longer," he continued, "because I rolled with Tom for about ten minutes after."

BJJ was all about defending yourself and submitting your opponent on the mats. It wasn't karate. There were no kicks, only standing up long enough to take someone to the ground. So when two people practiced their ground fighting, they called it rolling.

I glanced back at Harper, impressed. Intrigued. Something.

Since she didn't seem to be afraid of Jack and was completely ignoring Jimmy, I had to wonder why she was so scared of *me*.

I was a punk, that was why. I also had a dark past. She *should* be scared of me. We might live in the same building, but we came from different sides of the tracks. Hell, completely different worlds. If she was a professor, that meant she was smart as shit. I barely got my GED, and that had been in juvie. Yeah, different worlds.

Then there was Larry. Larry the Loser who sauntered over to stand beside her treadmill. He was a lawyer and thought he was tough shit. Too bad for him he wasn't and was trying to bag Harper. We couldn't hear what they said, but I had to hope her reply to his blatant proposition was "back off, asshole." Why he thought the middle of her run was when to ask her out only proved he was a total douche bag.

"If Larry fucks with her, I want to know about it," I told Jack, my tone serious.

He nodded. "Yeah, no problem."

Gray came out of his office to stand beside us, arms crossed over his chest. The doc's kid stormed past and out the door.

"If you're good here for a minute," Jack said. "I'll go get the towels out of the dryer."

Gray offered him a nod, and Jack went into the back.

"Are you okay?" he asked, eyeing me. His dark eyes were shrewd. He wore fighter shorts and a gym t-shirt, flip flops. Since no shoes were allowed on the mats or in the ring, he only wore sneakers for working out. But no one would take him for anything less than a total badass. Yeah, he had tattoos. Yeah, he had the close-cropped hair, the broken nose, the mangled fighter hands. Yet he was known for being a cowboy. Dressing like one with snap shirts and a fucking Stetson. He'd grown up on a ranch in Wyoming. The place was his hell on Earth, and as far as I knew, he'd never gone back after he left for the army. He had his own spread now, closer. His retreat when he needed to check out for a while. Now, he and Emory spent weekends up there, riding horses and most likely fucking. So yeah, Gray was a killer in a cowboy hat. He wasn't called The Outlaw for nothing.

I felt like a Girl Scout when I stood next to him. Harper must have met him to check out the apartment, sign the lease, and I hadn't heard she'd freaked out over him. Somehow, it seemed Harper wasn't afraid of him, only me.

I put my hand up to my jaw, rubbed it. "I've been hit worse. I assume you're not taking him on." I was the sole full-time fighter he trained right now, but he did private sessions with many. I got paid to do a few as well. The kid would have had to take me out with more than a punch for Gray to replace me.

He only rolled his eyes in response. "Thought you'd have hit the showers by now."

I lifted my arm and sniffed. "That's what Jack said. Do I smell that bad?"

When he didn't say anything, just took stock of what was going on in the gym, I added, angling my chin toward the treadmills, "I met our new neighbor."

"Harper? Is that why you're standing here? Stalking her?"

I laughed, ran my hand over the back of my neck, felt the dried sweat. "I just ran into her a few minutes ago." I left out the details. The fact that she freaked wasn't something I was going to tell. I could ask him if he knew her issues, but again, I didn't feel like being a fucking gossip. I never pulled that shit, and I wasn't starting now. No, she had a problem with me, and I needed to find out what it was. Yeah, I was pretty fucking scary. An asshole, too. But never to her. She just had to stand still long enough for me to prove it to her.

"Emory texted. Dinner at eight at our place. Harper's invited, too." He leaned in, sniffed. Grinned. "If you don't want to scare her off, I'd shower first."

Fucker.

Pushing off the counter, I walked out of the gym, knowing I didn't even need to smell bad to do that.

3

$\mathcal{H}$ARPER

"Oh, hi," I stuttered when my neighbor opened the stairwell door. Since he was tugging on a black puffy coat, I'd surprised him. Again.

I frowned, confused. Where were Emory and Gray? This was the door to their apartment.

He quickly stepped back, and I realized he was doing that to give me room, lots of room, so I wouldn't freak again. He even put his hands out at his sides, palms toward me, to show me he wasn't going to grab me. Shame filled me, and I felt my cheeks flush hotly.

I'd run longer than anticipated. Thoughts of Cam, what he wanted, the mortifying way I'd panicked about my neighbor hadn't faded after the usual five miles. I'd wanted to run away from it all, perhaps metaphorically, so I'd kept going, pushing myself until my muscles quivered, sweat poured down my face, my brain finally numb. When

I'd finished, Jack, at the gym's front desk, handed me a note from Gray. An invitation to dinner. Quickly showering, I threw on a pair of jeans, ankle boots and a dark green sweater. My hair was barely dry before I went upstairs.

While the elevator opened to a central hallway on the floor I shared with Reed, it opened directly into the couple's apartment on the third floor, so only they could make the third-floor button work with their key passes. That meant taking the emergency stairs and knocking, which was perfectly fine with me although my legs screamed at the effort, even only going up one flight.

Reed offered me a small, tentative smile, and damn, he had a dimple. He'd cleaned up since the elevator fiasco. While he still had stubble on his jaw, he'd changed into a long sleeved t-shirt that matched his blue eyes—how had I missed the striking contrast to his dark hair?—and a pair of well-worn jeans. Wearing boots instead of flip flops, he was a half head taller than me. This time, without the all-consuming panic, I could see that while his tattoos were covered, he still gave off the street fighter vibe, yet his gaze was calm. His stance easy going. There was none of that *evil* lurking there I'd seen in the men who'd attacked me.

"Okay?" he asked, his voice low. Gentle.

From Gray and Emory's apartment, music was playing, set low. I didn't smell dinner, and from where I stood, couldn't see the dining room table set for eating. Were we alone?

I couldn't slink away and hide with embarrassment, no matter how much I wanted to. If I did, he'd probably think I was scared of him. Again. Still. I owed him an apology, so I nodded. Cleared my throat. "Yes, thanks. I promise not to freak out this time."

He only gave a quick nod as reply. "I should probably introduce myself," he said. "I'm Reed."

"Harper."

He held out his hand, and when he clasped mine, I could feel the rough callouses, the strength. I *should* feel afraid because I was well aware how easily he could hurt me. Guys like him weren't in my usual social circle. Gray was the first professional fighter I'd ever met, and I could only imagine what my mother would think of my new landlord —and neighbor. Either way, I wasn't scared of Reed. Not at all. Perhaps it was because we were standing in Emory's doorway or that I'd run seven miles and burned all my fear away. Perhaps it was because I felt something else entirely toward him—all because of the feel of his hand holding mine. It definitely wasn't fear now that I took a moment to look my fill. I was attracted to him. Every conscious woman would be. I had no doubt he had women flinging themselves at him.

He wasn't doing anything but looking at me with those intense eyes. Waiting.

"I'm really sorry about earlier," I told him as he released my hand. Was his eye color ocean blue? Ice. That was it. They were ice blue.

"Gray said I scare people away when I'm ripe with sweat after a workout, but I hadn't really believed him before."

God, he was sweet. He was giving me an excuse to push my earlier panic onto him. No, I'd own up to it. Besides, he hadn't smelled bad. If something had been pumping from him, it was pheromones not BO. While I'd been struck by a panic attack, I'd still picked up on how hot he was. And now, my ovaries were jumping for joy just standing in front of this hot bad boy.

Yeah, he was *all* bad boy and made my nipples hard. I

hadn't had this reaction to a guy in a long time. Perhaps ever. Perhaps it was time I reevaluated my social circle because I'd been missing out.

"It wasn't you," I said sheepishly.

He looked skeptical, especially when he arched one dark brow, and the corner of his full mouth tipped up.

"I have a problem with elevators," I admitted.

He stared at me for a few seconds, rubbed the back of his neck, offered a small smile. "Elevators?"

I nodded in confirmation. "Big problem."

"I was not expecting that answer. Claustrophobia?"

I offered a slight shrug. "Something like that," I provided, not wanting to tell him the real reason. Now that would scare *him* away. He thought I was crazy enough already. "What *were* you expecting?"

He shrugged, and I didn't miss the play of his muscles beneath his collar. "I'm a pretty scary guy, Harper." Pointing to his face, he continued, "This mug's been in lots of fights, most of them outside of the ring."

I imagined he held his own pretty well, but I got what he was saying. He was a bad boy. Had a history that wasn't homecoming king and graduate school.

"What do the other guys look like then?"

His smile slipped entirely.

God, I'd said the wrong thing. I'd just been joking.

"Some of them, not so good," he told me. "That's why you should be wary. Your first instincts about me may have been right."

Even though he'd scared the shit out of me earlier, I wasn't getting any danger vibes now. What had he done to make him feel I should stay away from him?

"Emory's a good judge of character," I countered, tucking

my hair behind my ear. His eyes followed my action. "Like I said, it wasn't you. It was the stupid elevator."

He stepped out into the stairwell with me, pulling the door to the apartment closed behind him. "Come on," he said, his voice echoing off the concrete walls.

I frowned. "Where are we going? Isn't Emory expecting us?"

He went down a step, looked over his shoulder, so we were eye level. In the fluorescent lighting of the emergency stairs, his hair looked almost black.

"We're going to pick up the pizza Gray called in. Just down the street." Reed angled with his chin. "Emory worked today, her third in a row in the ER, so she's in the shower." He leaned in. "I have a feeling Gray's in there with her."

I felt my cheeks heat again. I wasn't a prude, but I hadn't really thought of my neighbor getting it on with her fiancé before. That set me in motion, so I followed him down the three flights of stairs. My legs were a little rubbery from my run, and I grabbed the railing, so I didn't fall on my face.

"Wednesday's are her no-cook day," he said. "Kind of like Taco Tuesday."

He stopped at the bottom, held the door open to the lobby for me.

"I never had Taco Tuesday growing up," I admitted, walking past. Yeah, it was more like eat-what-the-cook-served kind of thing in my house. We *never* ate together; my parents were always at some kind of fundraiser or dinner at the country club, my brother in his room playing a video game. And tacos? My mother would never eat food with her hands or anything she considered *ethnic*.

"Me either."

Reed started to push open the door to the parking lot

then stopped. He shrugged out of his coat. "Here. It's cold out."

I stared at the jacket for a moment. It *was* cold out, and I had no idea how far "just down the street" meant. I hadn't grabbed a coat because I'd had no idea I would be leaving the building.

"Thanks," I murmured, pulling it on. It was big on me, proving Reed was not a small man, that he was so much larger than me. The sleeves hung down past my hands, and he reached down, grabbed the cuff and rolled it up. Did the same for the other side.

With the scent of him surrounding me—kind of a mixture of dark woods and soap, and the way he was taking care of me—made my heart stutter. God, he was sweet. And dangerous. No, he wouldn't hurt me, I was sure of that now, but I could fall for him. *That* was bad. Falling for someone meant letting them in, and letting them in meant only heartache. People left or did something stupid like sell me to drug dealers.

Yet I savored his attention, his remarkably gentle actions for one who considered himself bad to the core. I took a deep breath, let it out. He was just rolling up coat sleeves, not slaying a dragon.

I glanced up through my lashes, saw his intent gaze, watched it lower to my mouth. What was it about him? We'd been in each other's presence for less than two minutes—when I wasn't having a panic attack—and somehow, it was as if he could see into my soul. I imagined what it felt like to be opposite him in the ring, with all that focus squarely on his opponent. My heart stuttered, and I forgot to breathe. This man was dangerous to me. To my safely guarded emotions.

Sex was easy for me. Something to do with a guy for a

release. Quick with an easy orgasm to clear my mind and to feel something. For a few minutes, I wasn't numb, and my mind went blissfully silent. There was no sleeping over at their place. Definitely not at mine. When it came to sex, I was the guy. Wham, bam, thank you, sir. I didn't even mind a janitor's closet to get the deed done. I preferred it that way, somewhere only the most important bits were uncovered long enough to fuck. The release was all I looked for. No strings. No connections. But Reed?

Even after having a panic attack because of him, I felt a connection, which was insane. And chemistry? God, the man oozed testosterone, and I wanted him. There was no doubt he'd be good. He'd know just how to make me come hard. My pussy clenched at the thought. But he was complicated, and I didn't need that.

"Thanks," I murmured then turned to the door, breaking the spell.

The air was cold, that sharp snap of winter making me stuff my hands into the pockets. There was no snow, and we hadn't seen more than a dusting of the white stuff this year. It didn't seem like it would be a white Christmas although there was still time for things to change.

We walked in silence down the sidewalk. Reed stood on the street side, and I noticed he kept his pace slow to match my shorter legs. I wasn't tiny at five-eight, but still.

"I heard you're a professor," he commented. "Impressive."

I glanced up at him, but he looked forward, almost scanning the block.

"Impressive?"

A couple came out of a restaurant, and I stepped out of their way. Reed put his hand at my back, and I felt it through the soft layer of his coat as he guided me around them.

"I teach Art History and have been told it's really dry. Stuffy."

"You don't seem the stuffy type," he countered without delay, as if he hadn't taken time to consider.

"Oh?" I couldn't help but smile. "What's the stuffy type look like?"

I saw the corner of his mouth tip up. "Tweed jackets with arm patches. Old."

"That's more my English counterparts than me."

"You like to run." He switched topics as we stopped at an intersection, waited for the light to change. The wind kicked up when a car sped by.

"I do. Good exercise." And stress relief.

"I run as part of my training," he said, glancing down at me. "But I hate it. I do it for the endurance and only three miles at a time."

"But then you do other things... as part of your workout. I mean, it takes a lot to win those matches."

I hadn't known who he was at the time, but I'd seen him once at the gym. He'd made my head turn. He'd been in a class and someone was demonstrating a skill, so everyone had been sitting on the mat watching. He'd had his eyes on the teacher, and I'd had my eyes on him because... wow. I hadn't been around when he trained with Gray or got in the ring and fought. Emory had said they trained in the early mornings. That was definitely *not* my time to work out.

He shrugged. "You teach. I fight."

We stopped in front of a pizzeria, and he held the door open for me. The scent of garlic and marinara sauce surrounded us as we entered the crowded restaurant. It was warm from the ovens and the windows were a little fogged. It was casual, low key and my stomach rumbled. After my seven-mile run, I needed calories. Gooey, cheesy calories.

"This is your job then, fighting. It's not a hobby for you."
He shook his head.

"Surely, you're more than just a fighter," I replied, having to raise my voice over the din.

I joined him in the line at the take-out counter.

He glanced down at me, eyes roving over my face, dropping to my lips for a moment. "Nah, I'm just a fighter." He held up his hands, showed me the big knuckles, blunt fingers. "Always have been. That's all I know."

I wasn't so sure about that, but I didn't say anything.

"Everything I learned came from the streets not books. I see you as a prep school kid."

"That would be me," I told him. There was no reason to deny it because it was true. "Went to a fancy place in Denver."

It was a fancy coed private school that required uniforms and a huge chunk of cash for tuition. My parents had the means and the expectations that came with that kind of program although while I'd gone on to Cornell, an Ivy League school, I'd chosen to study art history, a complete disappointment to them.

What else was new?

"Prep school, then college, right? You have a PhD?"

I nodded.

"In what?"

"Medieval and Byzantine art specializing in gothic architecture."

It was a mouthful, and his eyebrows winged up.

"Impressive," he said slowly. "My fights? Let's just say I'm getting my PhD in fighting."

"When's your next competition?" I asked. The people in front of us took their pizza box and left. We stepped up to the counter, waited for one of the busy workers to come over.

"Fight," he explained. "January."

That wasn't far off, only a few weeks, and the idea of him in the ring made me nervous for him. "I'll come watch, but you have to win."

He looked down at me with a sly smile, but his eyes didn't meet mine, they were squarely focused on my mouth. "I always win. Especially when it's a hard fight."

I swallowed, thinking he might not be talking about MMA any longer.

"Hi, Reed." The counter girl interrupted us and gave Reed a very bright smile. "It's been a while." And a perfect view of her breasts in her snug t-shirt. The restaurant logo stretched snugly across her ample curves. She was probably twenty-one, blonde and smart in a way I never could be.

There were book smarts, which I had, then street smarts. Reed was all street smarts, I was sure, and this girl would be considered a genius. She knew the game. By putting her forearms on the counter and leaning in, she flaunted her assets. It screamed *I'm available*. I was always impressed by women who used what they had to get what they wanted. I saw nothing wrong with it, even envied them a bit for the skill, but this time, it only made me mad.

I was standing right next to Reed—we'd even been talking—and she knew I was with him. I was even wearing his damn coat. She didn't care. I had to wonder if their familiarity extended beyond pizza carry out. I shut that thought down because I didn't really want to go there.

"Hey, Claire. Yeah, not too much pizza during training." He patted his flat stomach. I wasn't sure if he knew her by name because he'd gotten friendly with her for a reason I was trying not to think about or because he actually did eat a lot of pizza and was lying out his ass.

"I'll be at your next fight." She flashed him a bright smile then bit her lip.

I barely suppressed an eye roll.

"Yeah? That's great," he replied without any feeling.

"Think there are any openings for a ring girl?"

And there it was. She wanted something from him, and it wasn't his brain. Nor his dick. Well, she probably wanted that, too, but she wanted his connections. She wanted a job as one of the women who, during a fight, walked around the outside of the ring carrying a sign with the round number on it. They wore minimal clothing, and her boobs would look perfect in the skimpy outfit.

She had no interest in him. It was fine to work connections to find a job, but she did it in the wrong way. Flirting with a guy to get a job only pissed me off since it only made her look stupid. Made it so a guy thought a woman could only get a job by flaunting her sexuality not her brains.

"Are the pizzas ready?"

He hadn't answered her question, and the way her coy smile slipped, she'd noticed, too.

"Yeah, let me check."

When she turned to grab the two boxes, bending down to retrieve them from a rack, her ass stuck straight out. It was a nice ass, damn her. Even running fifty miles or more a week, I didn't have an ass like that. If I tossed a coin at it, it would definitely bounce right off.

Reed just sighed and looked away.

We were quiet on the walk back to our building. I was thinking about how he must have girls flinging themselves at him, some, like Claire, wanting him for their own gain. If there hadn't been a counter separating them, I had no doubt she'd have jumped his bones if there was a chance he'd hook her up with that ring girl job. He didn't seem all that interested, so maybe he had a girlfriend.

Of course, he did. He was gorgeous and a gentleman, no matter what he thought of himself.

I was a stuffy university professor who studied seven-hundred-year-old cathedrals and was afraid of elevators. I definitely didn't have a ring girl's body. I had boobs, but not the right cup size for the job or a guy like Reed.

4

EED

HARPER HAD the sexy librarian thing down. Fuck.

I had no idea that prim shit worked for me. It was eight in the morning, and I was in the gym jumping rope, ten minutes into my stint based on the timer on the wall. She caught my eye through the windows to the parking lot. Yeah, she wore a knee length black coat and only an inch or two of her skirt's hem showed beneath. Her hair was pulled back into a simple, sleek ponytail, and I saw a glint of diamond at her ears. She was gorgeous in that expensive, elegant way. She didn't go flashy, no bedazzled shit. No tousled hair. She looked... effortless. It was her shoes that had me practically panting. Damn. She looked all prim and proper except for her four-inch heels.

Were all professors of medieval art this fucking hot? I had to wonder how many college boys filled her classes and had their dicks get hard just listening to her talk about stained glass windows and flying buttresses. Yeah, I'd looked that shit up online before I went to bed.

I wanted her to turn her fierce dark gaze on me, tell me I'd been a bad boy for talking in class and shut me up the only way she knew how—by sliding up the hem of that pencil skirt, climbing in my lap and taking me for a ride.

Fuck. I got a hard on just watching her unlock her car. That was something that had never happened to me before while jumping rope.

No, she wasn't stuffy. No fucking way.

Gray came over, followed the direction of my staring and glanced out the window. While he might be my trainer and made me suffer on a daily basis, he worked out with me every morning. We'd already run our usual three-mile circuit on the streets, done a few rounds in the ring, and I was cooling down with thirty minutes of jump rope. It was mindless, so I couldn't think of a better way to make the time pass than to watch my sexy neighbor leave for work.

The pizza had worked out well the night before. Besides it being low key and easy for Emory since she'd worked in the ER all day, it had given me the chance to talk with Harper alone. Taking her with me to pick up the order had made it casual. No expectations. But when she'd put on my coat and I saw how damn small she was in comparison to me, every protective instinct I had came out. I wanted to wipe away all her fear, to keep her safe, even from elevators or whatever the fuck happened to her to make her so damned scared of them.

With Gray and Emory, Harper had been funny and witty and relaxed as we all talked, but she didn't come out and say why she was afraid of elevators. Not that I'd expected her to, but it would have explained a lot. Claustrophobia? Trapped once? Free fall?

At first, I'd assumed it was a lie, a lie to hide the fact that she really was scared of me. But as we'd walked to the pizza place, I hadn't seen a hint of fear in her eyes. If she really was afraid of me, she'd have bolted again, not let me put my hand on the small of her back as we walked down the street. No, I'd seen surprise and interest instead. That interest, that spark of heat had me feeling, *shit*, something. She was gorgeous. She turned heads, especially mine, which was a fucking problem. Yeah, I wanted to get in her pants. Half the guys in the gym probably did after seeing her in those running shorts.

But that wasn't it. She was interesting and quirky. Who the hell got a doctorate in some obscure art topic? I wanted to know how she liked her coffee, whether she liked the beach or the mountains and whether she preferred satin or lace.

She wasn't the kind of girl to fuck and forget. She was more, and that was bad. I didn't want *more*.

Hell, even if I did, I couldn't. I was wrong for her. A bad choice. A dead end. If she knew my past, she'd all but sprint away from me. She was smart as fuck, gorgeous and deserved the whole two and a half kids and the dog and the picket fence shit. She deserved everything. And I was nothing.

That didn't mean I couldn't look and couldn't wonder, couldn't imagine pressing her over the hood of her car and sliding into her hot pussy. I groaned at the thought then quickly hid that sound from Gray with a cough.

She tossed her bag onto the passenger seat and climbed in, started her car.

"What's up with Harper?" I asked, lifting my chin in her direction. I was breathing hard but even. I wasn't too worn down that I couldn't hold a conversation as I kept pace.

Sweat dripped down my temples, and there was no way I could wipe it away. I had my rhythm, the plastic rope clacking on the concrete floor.

Gray shrugged, leaned against the wall and crossed his arms. He wore his usual T-shirt—stained with sweat—and fighter shorts, plus his running shoes. No one would know by looking at him in the gym he preferred snap shirts and cowboy hats. After a quick head tilt to the guy who came through the door, he replied, "Emory won't say."

This answer meant he, too, knew something was up. I hadn't told him about the elevator freak out.

While I appreciated Emory's ability to keep secrets like a bank vault, it would be really helpful to be able to figure Harper out. Was it claustrophobia? Obviously, she wasn't bothered by being in a car. Did that mean she wouldn't like to have her wrists pinned as she fucked?

I blew out a deep breath at the idea of having her beneath me. *Shit.* I was in trouble.

"I do know she's got issues with her family and was looking for a new place to live that was safe."

"Safe?" I asked, wondering what that meant. Safe, as in, the house was falling down or safe, like her mother was a serial killer?

"After the incident at Emory's house last summer." He bit off the words remembering what happened. Some lunatic had been beating up women for their pain pills, and Emory, who volunteered as a nurse practitioner at a family clinic, got in the guy's way. He'd broken into her house to mess with her, and she'd escaped by climbing down a fucking rope ladder. I'd been there when Gray got to her. While she hadn't been hurt, it had been a bad situation, and no doubt she had nightmares. Gray probably, too. If Harper had lived on the same street, it was likely she'd worried for her own safety after that.

"I thought maybe that was the reason, but when Emory mentioned a whack family, I started to think differently," he added.

"Everyone's got a crazy family," I countered. I didn't really have parents as much as fucking criminals who'd spawned me. They were dead, so that made things simpler. I seriously doubted Harper's mom was a drug addict, and her father made her be his getaway driver in armed robberies. No, probably her only parental problem as a kid was to worry if her parents would show up for her field hockey game. She was a princess.

Gray only arched a brow at my response, and I remembered the shit with his dad. Now *he* was an asshole. He owned Green Acres, a bunch of retirement communities all across the West. He might be successful, but he was a piece of work. A kid beater and worse.

Gray looked away from the window and focused on me. "All I know is, watch out for her."

I stopped the jump rope, even with time left, let it hang down in front of me. I took a deep breath, then another, wiped the back of my hand over my temple to catch the dripping sweat. "You think someone's trying to hurt her?"

Not on my fucking watch.

He shrugged, pushed off the wall. Grabbing his towel from a nearby bench, he wiped it over his sweaty head. "Perhaps, but while she can run faster and farther than anyone I've ever seen, sometimes you can't escape your problems. I think she's got some stuff she's working on."

Somehow, I had a feeling he wasn't talking about elevators.

5

$\mathcal{H}$ARPER

"DID you get a new outfit for the holiday party?" Sarah asked. She stuck her head in my office door, her eyes wide with female glee at the idea of a new outfit.

"I won't be here," I replied, glancing up at her.

I sat behind my desk, piled high with papers that needed to be graded and notes from the latest article I was writing on the use of the Latin Cross layout in later cathedral structures in northern Europe. It was the last week of the semester, and everyone was in the chaos and insanity of exams before the long winter break. Instead of going to the department holiday party this weekend, I was going to the UK. I had to do research for my latest paper that was being published, and the only free time I had from school was between semesters.

The excitement slipped from her face. "That's right. I forgot." Then she smiled again, sighed. "God, a vacation in

England. You can meet up with that guy, what's his name? Giles?"

Giles. A professor at the university in London, or lecturer as he was called in the UK. A one-night stand I'd told Sarah about. I may have embellished him a bit more than what it really was. We'd hit it off then gotten off in the supply closet on the third floor of the arts building. I hadn't lingered and hadn't seen him since. I barely thought about him.

But, Sarah was little Miss Matchmaker, and having a *possible* boyfriend in another country allowed me to string her along and keep any blind dates she might scrounge up from happening. I let her think Giles and I emailed each other and did stuff when I was in the UK, which was fairly often.

"Right. Giles," I replied.

"You'll be there for Christmas, won't you? If not, you'll come over."

She was married, had two kids who were in elementary school and a white Labrador whose shedding hair clung to all of Sarah's clothes. Going to her house for Christmas dinner would be a three-ring circus and remind me of a family life I never had.

"I will be away, yes," I replied vaguely.

"Dinner with Giles and his family?" she asked hopefully.

More like dinner with the flight attendants on the transatlantic flight coming home. I'd specifically planned my return for Christmas day. I hated the holiday. It was a day for family, and I had none. The day I'd been attacked was the day I severed all ties with them. They hadn't come to the ER to check on me, to sit with me as I spoke to the detectives. A few weeks later, they'd bailed Cam out of jail. Supporting him—no, trying to save him—when he'd been caught by undercover police selling drugs. I'd been dramatic and attention seeking. As if.

That had been it for me. I'd not once reached out to them, but that hadn't stopped them from contacting me, solely for selfish reasons.

I should be thankful for my friends, who were kind to include me, but it wasn't the same as family. It never would be, so I'd found ways to make Christmas just disappear. And while my research trip to England had been planned for the school winter break, I'd made sure I wasn't at home, anywhere really, for the actual holiday.

"We'll see," I replied. "What are you wearing to the party?"

My question redirected her as I'd hoped, and I listened as she spoke of the new top she bought that required new shoes to go with it.

"I have those chandelier earrings you can borrow." My phone rang from beneath the papers.

Sarah rolled her eyes and gave me a wave as I dug it out then answered.

"Harper Lane."

"Your brother is reaching out to you, Harper."

God.

I couldn't look at Sarah, so I just gave her a vague wave in return and spun my chair around to face the wall. It may have been a little rude, but I wouldn't let my friend see my face. Not now. Seven words from my mother, and I was destroyed. I stared blindly at the large cork board filled with photos I'd taken of various cathedrals across Europe as well as paintings I lectured on. Close ups of mosaic tiles and examples of pristine stained glass.

I saw none of it. My lunch became unsettled. All because of *her.*

"Yes, I've heard from him," I replied. My voice was monotone. I had nothing to give to my mother, no emotion. *Nothing.* After what she'd done, I was a dry well. It had been six months since she called me last, when Cam had been hurt in a fight in the prison yard. Why she'd called me to tell me about it, I had no idea. She called now because Cam had tried yesterday and failed to get me to engage.

"He's in jail. The least you can do is be responsive."

I pulled the phone away from my head, stared at it. "He gave me to drug dealers as payment, Mother." The fact I had to remind her of this made it instantly clear she was not calling for reconciliation. "I have nothing to say to him." *Or you.*

"That... *incident* is not why he is in jail—therefore, you should empathize with his plight."

He'd gotten away with my assault since the men who'd attacked me were never found. And, my parents' lawyer had done a great job of ripping me apart to the D.A. to save Cam. Even so, he'd done something else stupid—which, like she said, had nothing to do with me—and ended up in jail anyway.

I let my head fall forward, closed my eyes. "What do you want?"

"He will be released on the twenty-third. A wonderful Christmas present. We are having a little party with his friends. Seven-thirty. You will come and—"

"No." The single word was like a bullet. "I will not come. I will not talk with him. I will not talk with you. Goodbye."

Spinning around, I slammed the phone down just as I hit my knee on the inside of my desk.

"Fuck," I breathed, wincing and taking deep breaths to ease the pain, rubbing at the abused bone.

Slowly, my knee felt better, but my heart didn't. What

the fuck was wrong with my family? Why couldn't they just be normal, nice people instead of sociopaths? I wanted to throw up. I wanted to swipe all the papers off my desk. I wanted to scream.

I couldn't do any of that. Not here, not now. Looking up at the clock on the wall, I had a full afternoon of exams. I could run this off. Later. Or fuck it all away. Yeah, that would be good. The connection with someone else, even for a little bit. An orgasm was like a hit of some hard drug.

The alarm on my cell went off, a daily reminder of my first afternoon class. Fuck. I took a deep breath. Another. Thought of the wall my therapist had told me to visualize. To build it brick by brick around my anger and frustration at my family, at what happened to me, until it was completely walled off. The concept was great, but it didn't really work. Still, I tried.

I had students waiting to take their semester final on triptych paintings and clerestory windows. Teaching was soothing although exam time was a little hectic. The familiarity of my subject matter was almost comforting. Seven-hundred-year-old cathedrals didn't talk back, didn't fuck up your life. They were consistent, enduring. They were always there. The same, familiar, no matter what shit came your way.

6

EED

"WORD ON THE STREET, you're going down," Gray said. He leaned back in his desk chair, fingers steepled in front of him. He was in jeans and t-shirt with the gym logo on the chest. His Stetson was in its usual spot on the hook behind his desk. He wore the serious expression of a guy in ruthless control but would much rather beat the shit out of something. Or someone. In this case, I knew who it was.

"Dominguez."

It wasn't the guy I was fighting next week. He was clean. Or at least he'd be clean in the ring. It was his backers, one of them specifically. Instead of having sponsors who touted the latest protein powder or sneaker, Sammy the Sandbag Briggs had Dominguez who was infamous for leading one of the nastier gangs in the area, including as far away as Denver. With Brant Valley's crime rate only getting worse, it only proved he was one mean fucker.

"How the hell did Sammy get mixed up with him?" I asked, shaking my head. I knew the rough life of the streets, the way things worked, but the shit I'd done didn't even approach what Dominguez did.

"I've heard Sammy's sister is baby mama for one of Dominguez's men."

"Baby mama?" I asked, stunned he'd use that term.

"What? I know my street language." Gray offered a quick smile then let it fall away. "I don't think Sammy's got much choice in who's backing him."

"I thought he had that energy bar company taking him out for dinner."

"That was before Dominguez got his hands on him. Everything's changed now."

I could only imagine. Sammy must be shitting himself over this whole thing. Would they kill him if he lost the fight next month?

"So Dominguez will bet on the fight, make some cash," I said, dummying it down.

"If you lose," he added, leaning forward, putting his forearms on his desk.

I looked at Gray. We didn't have to say anything because I wasn't throwing the fight, and I wasn't losing. Fuck no. I couldn't worry about Sammy's neck with only a few weeks to go.

A tap on the office window had me turning around. When Jack caught my eye, he tilted his head past the front counter. I looked in that direction and saw Harper walking out of the gym with Larry the Loser.

"What the fuck?" I muttered.

Harper was in her work clothes. I wouldn't forget those hot heels. She wasn't in the gym for exercise. No. Based on the look on Larry's face, she'd taken him up on his offer for a quick fuck. I'd heard his lines, and no woman I'd ever met went for it. He was probably zero for fifty. I'd seen for myself the way she'd turned him down the day before. Obviously not. I didn't give a shit who Larry fucked except Harper.

I stood and walked out of Gray's office without looking back. "Later."

If Gray wanted to talk more, he'd have to wait. There was no way in hell I was letting Larry get his hands on her.

I walked past Jack, who had a pile of clean towels in front of him to fold, and out into the lobby. No Harper. No Larry. I glanced out into the parking lot. Empty. She wouldn't take the elevator to her apartment, which meant—

Pulling out my key pass from my pocket, I slapped it against the wall sensor, then opened the heavy door to the emergency stairs. There, against the concrete wall, was Harper. Larry was looking down at her and stroking his knuckles along her upper arm. The scene was fucking odd. Larry in his workout clothes, a white muscle shirt and black shorts. He was gangly and had curly hair that was like a dark mop on top of his head—and on his chest. He had the physique of a runner; no amount of weight lifting would get him to bulk up.

For a guy, he wasn't hideous, but his personality was of a dead fish. A dead fish who wanted to get in the pants of any woman who was conscious. He might even try for ones who weren't.

They whipped their heads in my direction when I interrupted them. Harper didn't have the look of a woman who wanted to fuck. No heated gaze, no lip biting or flushed cheeks, no aggressive hands. She just looked stunned to see me.

Larry straightened, turned to face me. "Reed, I was just—"

"Leaving," I said, finishing for him. Crossing my arms over my chest, I stared him down. I didn't want to lay him out, but I would if he didn't step the fuck away from Harper.

He lifted his hands as if he were being robbed. "Hey, she propositioned me."

I clenched my fists. Wrong answer. He was putting this whole thing on Harper. Yeah, he was a sucker for a beautiful woman, but she hadn't been leading him out of the gym by his dick. I didn't give a shit if a woman wanted to fuck. It was her prerogative as much as any guy, but Larry didn't have to be a douchebag about it. Shaming Harper wasn't the way to get beneath that pencil skirt.

Larry narrowed his eyes and studied me then looked to Harper then back. "Are you—"

"Going to kill you?" I asked, my voice taking on an edge it didn't have before. "That's up to you."

His eyebrows rose to disappear beneath his hair. He sighed, dropped his hands to his sides and moved past me to open the door. "Sorry, my bad."

I didn't watch him leave, only waited for the heavy slam to know we were alone.

Harper wouldn't look at me. Her hands were flat against the concrete wall at her sides, as if it was holding her up.

I looked her over, took in her prim work clothes, the way her hair fell forward to shield her face. "Do you really want him, Harper?"

She turned to me, narrowed her dark eyes. "You have no right."

"If you really want to fuck Larry, I'll go back and get him. Even apologize." I paused, but she didn't respond. "Do you want me to do that?"

She pursed her lips. "No."

"You want to fuck?" I put a hand on my chest. "I'm right here."

Her mouth fell open, and she looked at me in outrage. She didn't need to use fists to take me down, just that glare.

"I don't want to—"

"Then what were you doing with Larry?"

"I...I—" She looked away, knowing I'd caught her in her own lie. "Just leave me alone."

She started to climb the stairs, but I grabbed her wrist before she made it far.

"Oh, no. You approached Larry for a reason." I tugged her, so she turned and faced me. With her on the steps, she was a few inches taller than me. "Does he make you wet, princess?"

Her cheeks flushed, and she pulled against my hold. If Larry didn't make her hot, then why did she go to him?

"I'm not answering that," she snapped. Every line in her body was filled with tension. I had to assume she knew no self-defense, otherwise she'd have broken my nose by now or worse, kneed me in the nuts. I turned my hips a little though, just in case.

"Because the answer is no. You wanted to fuck him but weren't interested."

"What's wrong with that?" she countered, clearly offended. "What's wrong with a woman wanting a quick release?"

"Absolutely nothing." The idea of seeing Harper come, hearing the sounds she'd make, made me hard. "You want to get off."

When she just crossed her arms and stared down at me with that stern librarian look, I'd had enough.

I stepped up, leaned in and tossed her over my shoulder.

I didn't slow as I went up the stairs, even when she pummeled my back. I only set her down when we were in my apartment, door locked behind us.

I sat down in my overstuffed armchair, took her hand and pulled her to stand before me. The apartment was sparsely furnished. I didn't need much. There were no knick-knacks from trips, no family photos. Yeah, my dad never let me stop the car for a selfie together after he robbed a convenience store. No framed prints on the walls. I didn't bring women here, so there was no one to impress.

After a long day of training, I liked to sit in my chair in front of the TV, zone out or even ice something that needed it. While it wasn't my bed, it was a close second. And having Harper stand before me... hell. Just having her in the apartment changed the feel of the place.

I didn't release her hand but tugged her close, my knees parted, so she was right there. If I leaned forward, I could put my mouth on her breast.

She was pissed. Really pissed. Perhaps she knew she couldn't win against a fighter. Perhaps she was just being patient and waiting for a moment to strike—or slip away. It was a smart move for an uneven fight, and I figured this was more her plan. But I wasn't going to let that happen. She wasn't going anywhere until I had this figured out. Until I had *her* figured out.

"I'll get you off," I promised. "Come closer."

Giving her a tug, she gasped as she fell forward, her hand landing on my shoulder for balance. Her one knee settled on the outside of my thigh. Her skirt was narrow, so she hovered above me somewhat awkwardly.

"Reed," she practically growled, trying to retreat.

My hands cupped her thighs just above her knees and

slid the material of her skirt up until she could settle herself, straddling my legs. I was used to a willing woman on my lap. Harper resisted and cried out my name again, and it wasn't in pleasure.

I studied her closely. I'd let her go if she was really freaked. Right now, she was just mad. I could handle that. I needed to know what was going on in that gorgeous head of hers. She was probably one of the smartest people I knew, yet she'd been ready to fuck Larry. It made no sense.

"I don't want to have sex," she told me, making it clear she was saying no. I saw the crease that formed in her brow, heard her angry tone. I still didn't let her up.

"Oh? You wanted it downstairs. Is it me? I just don't do it for you?" The sarcastic lilt to my voice didn't go unnoticed.

A sigh escaped as she glared at me. "Just leave me alone."

"No can do, princess."

Her palm pushed against my chest, as if that would help her. The feel of her small hand made my dick hard, but I willed it down. Now wasn't the time to play.

"Stop calling me that."

I flicked my gaze to meet hers. "Compared to me, you're a princess."

She rolled her eyes. "Whatever. I'm just going to go to my apartment."

With one hand on her thigh, I kept her in place. "If you don't give a shit about Larry, why were you going to let him fuck you?"

"Do you give a shit about every woman you're with?" she countered, the words fired like bullets. I wasn't going to answer that. It was a double standard with what men got away with, but this wasn't about her sex life. It was about her safety. I had size and weight on my side, plus my ability to fight. I could protect myself. Harper was easy prey for an asshole who wanted more than she was willing to give, especially if she were the one doing the offering.

"I saw the way the girl at the pizza place was with you," she continued. "Don't tell me you didn't fuck a groupie after some match and never see her again."

"I won't." I wouldn't lie to her. I'd fucked women and forgotten their names directly after. A few I hadn't even *known* their names. "But you're not me. A quickie isn't your style."

"Are you sure? You don't even know me."

"I know enough. You wouldn't do this unless—"

I stopped the rest of the sentence because it all made sense. All at once, I knew, and I saw her in a completely different way. It wasn't about the sex.

"It's about the release," I said, my voice calm. Quiet. "You want to come, to feel good, even just for a moment. To forget, don't you?"

She looked over my shoulder, color brightening her cheeks. Her shoulders went up. Yeah, I'd hit a nerve, and that meant I was getting close to the truth.

"Had a rough day? Tell me about it." I gave her thighs a little squeeze, ignored how soft her skin felt. How supple the toned flesh was.

"Why?"

I cocked my head, studied her. "Because I like you, and I want to know."

"No." I felt her body stiffen, watched as her shoulders went back. She shook her head, her hair falling in front of her face again. She ruthlessly tucked it behind her ears. "I don't want to talk. I want to fuck, but I don't do relationships."

"So, Larry then. As for relationships? Good. Neither do I."

I wanted to be honest with her. I'd kill for a relationship with someone like her, but no. I wasn't that much of an asshole. I wasn't going to bring her down into my world. She deserved so much more. She already *was* so much more.

When she wiggled her hips, I let go of my hold. She slithered back and lowered to her knees, looked up at me through her lashes. Shit. Harper on the floor between my legs was fucking hot, and my dick throbbed. The idea of those pouty lips stretched wide around it had me stifling a groan. When her hands slid up my thighs, I knew once she succeeded in her task of getting my dick out, I wouldn't have any more control.

"No." The word came out sharper than I wanted, but hell, she was about to touch my dick. "You won't use a BJ to keep from talking."

Using my fighter strength, I tugged her back up onto my lap, her skirt riding up to her hips. My hands went back to her thighs.

"No?" she asked, her brow crinkled in a frown. "You don't want my mouth?"

"If I wanted to be serviced, I'd go to a whore. That's not you, Harper."

Angry fire filled her eyes, her cheeks flushing. "How dare—"

"No," I said again. "You want my attention? You crave being with someone? That's fine. I'll even get you off. But not like this."

"Fine, we'll fuck," she snapped.

My thumbs slid back and forth over her inner thighs. Slowly, I moved them closer and closer to her pussy which was covered in a thin scrap of pale pink silk and lace. Good thing my dick was still in my pants. It was the only way to keep from busting a nut. The fabric clung to her folds, which were clearly outlined by the damp silk. I wanted to touch what was beneath, to feel her heat, her wetness, learn how soft she'd be. But not today.

"No fucking," I countered.

All I did was brush my thumbs over the delicate edges of her panties, back and forth.

"Reed," she murmured, letting her eyes fall closed.

Fuck. I could come from just that sound, the feel of her, the sight of her panties, the scent of her.

"You want to come?" I whispered.

She didn't open her eyes, just nodded her head. Bit her lip.

Moving my right thumb an inch, I moved it over her clit. I didn't press down, just brushed over it through her panties. I wanted answers, and I was going to get them. A pliant and mindless Harper was the only way she was going to open up.

"Why Larry?"

I waited, let her sink more into her clit being stroked. Asked again.

"He... he offered the other day. He's easy."

That was true. He was a total man whore.

"Why didn't you come to me?"

When she didn't answer, I stroked over her panties a little faster. I watched her face, learned what made her hot.

"I... I don't know you."

Bad answer. "You don't know Larry. Why, princess?"

She whimpered when I stilled my thumb.

"Why?"

She licked her lips. "Because you're not easy. Because I would want more."

I wasn't sure if I should be thrilled or disappointed, but I rewarded her with a slip of my thumb.

"Yes," she hissed.

"You're a good girl, princess. You deserve more than a fuck in a stairwell."

She shook her head, her eyes squeezed shut. "I don't want it."

"Yes, you do. You crave being with someone. You deserve more than a mindless release. You deserve an even exchange." And her on her knees before me, sucking my dick wasn't an even exchange. "A connection."

Her head moved back and forth, continuing to deny my words. I loved the way her hair fell over her shoulders, the way her skin flushed. "No. No! It's too painful. I won't get close."

The left side of her clit seemed to be more sensitive, so I focused my attentions there. Slowed my thumb to brush over just that small point. I ached for her, to hear the truth of her feelings, to know she felt she had to debase herself to the point of fucking a guy like Larry just to feel good.

"Who hurt you?"

A tear slid down her cheek. Shit. I'd found the problem, but it wasn't something I could fix. She didn't get a flat tire or a reprimand from her boss. She was upset about the past, something bigger than a bad day.

"Tell me who hurt you, and I'll let you come."

She shifted her hips, starting to take what she wanted, to move into the pleasure, and all I did was touch her through her panties. "My... my family."

I wanted to stop, to hear what they'd done, but I couldn't deny her the release she craved. I worked her with my thumb until her nails dug into my shoulders, until her head fell back, her long hair dangled down her back, her neck vulnerable and exposed.

Fuck, she was gorgeous, and I wanted to watch her come more than anything else in my life. "Come, princess."

She did, and I felt her thighs quiver as they pressed into mine, watched her breasts rise and fall beneath her blouse as she cried out her release, felt her panties become wet from a flood of her desire. It was the most beautiful thing I'd ever seen, and that unsettled me. I'd never been affected like this before, and I'd only touched her over her panties, and my dick was tucked away—painfully—in my jeans. How had something so... so high school seemed like something new?

She was as broken as me. Money and privilege, opportunity even, didn't keep someone from bad shit. The night before she'd mentioned having a shitty family, and whatever happened between them cut her deep. Some people drank, some did drugs. Some did reckless shit like skydiving to ease the pain. It seemed Harper lost herself in meaningless sex.

She was done with that. Larry was the last loser she pulled into a stairwell to make herself feel better.

I continued to stroke her until the last bits of her pleasure ebbed. Her eyes opened, met mine. Instead of a sated smile, her eyes widened as if she just realized what she'd done, and then she crumbled. She started to cry. Her hands covered her face as she straddled me and sobbed. For a moment, I was frozen, completely surprised by the swift change, but I should have known.

She'd wanted a release, to come and feel better. Larry would have given it to her, but I doubted she'd have felt safe enough to let go completely. What she probably hadn't even realized was that she'd needed to cry, and Larry wouldn't have been able to give her that. I had. Because she trusted me, felt protected enough to let down every one of those damn walls. I felt humbled and in trouble. This woman was going to make me think things I could never have.

7

$\mathcal{H}$ARPER

THIS HADN'T GONE as I'd expected. I was sitting in Reed's lap crying, my skirt all but bunched about my waist.

I didn't cry. There hadn't been any tears left from two years ago. I'd thought they were all gone, but no. Somehow Reed—god, the one man I never expected—turned me into a damn faucet. All because he'd refused to fuck me.

I had no idea how long I cried. Minutes? Hours? The entire time, he just sat there and rubbed my back, my cheek pressed into his chest. He was warm, his big hands comforting, and I'd felt... protected. He'd allowed me to let my guard down, and he'd seen me at my worst. I could only imagine what he thought of me.

I sat up quickly, almost bumping his chin doing so. With my fingers, I wiped the tears from my cheeks. I was sure my mascara stained them. God, I probably looked a mess. "I'm sorry. I... I don't usually do that."

"No, I didn't think you did," he replied quietly.

I dared a peek at him, and I was surprised. He wasn't revolted or even bored. He looked concerned. It wasn't an expression I expected to see on a tough fighter. Those pale eyes had none of the cold fury he'd aimed at Larry. Only concern. Patience. Curiosity.

I sniffed, tried to push through my embarrassment. "I should go."

His hands were on my thighs again, this time the touch wasn't sexual but gentle. I could feel rough callouses, reminding me they were weapons against others. But not me. For me, his touch was gentle and comforting.

"Not yet. I can't let you leave like this." His voice was missing that sharp bite from before.

"I'm fine," I countered, taking a deep breath. I was calmer now, if only I could extricate myself from his lap, from his apartment and die of embarrassment alone. I'd gotten on my knees with the intention of sucking him off. My neighbor! I could never live that down, never look him in the eye again.

"You will be. Just give yourself a minute."

He was too damn patient. How did a brawler like him end up being so sweet? I didn't dare ask. I knew he'd been aroused. I'd felt his hard length press against me, and if I glanced down, I'd see the thick outline through his jeans. But he wasn't doing anything about it. Why?

"Don't you want me to..." I couldn't say the rest, just tilted my head down.

"Not tonight."

Not tonight? I frowned. "But this was just a one-time thing."

His pale eyes held mine as he reached up and stroked

my hair back from my face where it clung to my damp cheeks. "No way."

"But you don't want *more.*"

"I'm not looking for a relationship, no. But I won't have you getting your needs met by some random guy. He could be an asshole or worse. It's too dangerous. Like I said before, you come to me if you need to get off."

"Or cry," I said, shame faced.

"Or cry," he repeated. "A release is a release, princess. Feel better?"

I did. Yeah, what he'd done with his thumb had been just short of miraculous, and he'd barely touched me. I could only imagine what it would be like if we took our clothes off, were skin to skin. To say there was chemistry between us was an understatement.

It had just been his concern, his quiet presence that settled me. He knew now that I had some serious issues with my family, but who didn't? Fortunately, I hadn't told him about Cam or my mother. He hadn't known about my need for connection that my therapist called self-destructive. Well, he did now. And still, he wasn't judging, wasn't using me for himself. He'd declined a blow job. He could ask for me to get him off—it was his turn—but he didn't. He probably had the worst case of blue balls and didn't seem to care.

"I'm to just knock on your door, and we'll what... fuck?"

He arched a dark brow but didn't rise to my bait. I *was* trying to rile him, to see how far I could push him with this. It wasn't working. "One of these days, princess, I'll get inside you. When it's time."

His words made me shiver. I hadn't lied when I'd told him I'd want more if I were with him. And not just sex. He was dangerous to my carefully built walls. He'd already gotten past most of it; I didn't cry for anyone. Ever. If I let him, he'd knock it all down, and then I'd be vulnerable. I couldn't be hurt again. Couldn't be made worthless by those who should have cared.

I cocked my head to the side, studied him. "How do you fight in the ring when you're so damn chill?" I asked.

That got a smile from him. Just that tilt of his mouth, and his entire look changed. Gone was the hard ass, the ruthless competitor. He was rugged and so fucking handsome. My eyes dropped to those lips, wondered what a kiss would be like.

"I figured you to be a cowboy like Gray."

He shook his head. "I'm more than a cowboy, princess. I'm a fighter. That's my job. But you're not my opponent," he told me. "We'll do this together. I don't want a quick fuck with you. I want *more*. You're more, Harper, even if you don't believe it."

Something flipped inside my chest then, and it was in the vicinity of my heart. It had been walled off for so long that the sensation startled me. Scared me to feel it.

This time, when I tried to stand, he let me. I brushed down my skirt, thinking about how I'd been so lewdly displayed in his lap—even though I'd originally been there to fuck.

"I'm going to go." I glanced down at him, even as I ran my hands over my thighs to smooth the fabric. "Um, well, thank you."

He only nodded his head slightly as he stood and followed me to the door, opening it for me. I stepped out into the hallway, turned to face him.

"See you around." What did one say to a guy who'd turned you down for sex, got you off with his thumb and let you cry on him? When the corner of his mouth tipped up and made him seem less dangerous and wickedly handsome at the same time, I knew it was the right thing.

He waited until I had my door unlocked before he closed his. Reed, although he'd probably deny it, was a gentleman. A fighter, bad boy, gentleman.

After closing my door behind me, I flipped on the light, took in my unpacked apartment and felt a wave of loneliness. It was because I'd opened myself up and been vulnerable for Reed that I felt gutted. I wanted to crawl back on his lap and stay there. It would go away, this need for someone else. To be held, comforted. It had to. But how? The man who seemed to be seeing every one of my cracks lived ten feet away. He was getting too close and not just physically. I needed space, time to regroup, and I couldn't do it if I might run into him.

There was only one way to do it. Leave. My therapist would say avoidance wasn't the way to go, but she'd never met Reed, never come like I had with just his thumb over my panties. I grabbed my cell to pull up my plane reservation but almost dropped it when I saw the screen. I'd missed a call, and I recognized the number. My father's office. It hadn't changed in all the years he'd worked as partner in the law firm in Denver. My number, though, *had* changed. Several times in the past two years. There was only one way he'd gotten it.

Cam.

Fuck. They were all against me. Whatever tension I'd worked out of my body by Reed's diligent thumb or my crying jag was gone. I didn't want to talk to them. I didn't want to think about Cam getting out of jail or the way my parents enabled him. Fortunately, I wouldn't be in town—or the country even—on his release day. I just needed to get away from them, from whatever Reed had stirred up.

It wasn't fair to lump him in with my family. There was no comparison whatsoever. While my parents and brother brought up old emotions and ripped off scabs on barely healed mental scars, Reed was coming at me from a different direction, which was just as overwhelming. Perhaps even more so because I didn't understand it. I knew my parents. I knew Cam. I knew their strategy, and I had a plan in place to defend myself from their constant attacks. I had defenses, no matter how weak they were.

But Reed? I had a feeling he was going to be hard to fight.

There was an easy solution to get away from my family, at least a temporary one. To give me some space to think about Reed. I pulled up my reservation on the airline's app and changed it.

8

EED

I DIDN'T SEE Harper leave for work as I'd hoped. I'd barely slept, thinking about her. I'd had to take my dick in hand not once but twice to ease the ache for her. Remembering how she looked when she came finished me off in record time.

When Gray and I came back from our morning three-mile run, I noticed her car was gone from the parking lot. Yeah, I was taking note of her car like I was pussy whipped. Six-thirty was early to go to the office, but this was the last week of the semester—she'd shared that over pizza the other night—and her schedule was crazy busy.

Watching her walk in those sky-high heels she seemed to wear would have made my half hour of jump roping much more enjoyable. Instead, I'd thought about the feel of her toned thighs beneath my palms, the silk of her panties, the softness of her folds and swollen clit through that wet fabric. The way her eyes went from spitting fire to blurry passion. And the way she came for me from just my thumb, fuck, she was incredibly responsive. It had been the second day in a row I'd had a hard-on while jumping rope.

A woman's mind was something I never tried to figure out, but Harper's? Hell, she was complex. And she had some serious problems. Problems I wished I could solve for her, so I never had to see her cry again.

That had gutted me, and I'd had no idea how to make her feel better. One minute she was on her knees ready to suck my dick, the next she was coming in my arms then had tears streaming down her face.

I'd never had a woman sob in my lap before. For a few seconds, I'd been stunned. Confused, even. But she hadn't been crying because I'd hurt her or touched her in a way she didn't like. No, she'd cried because I gave her a safe place to do it. I'd pushed her just far enough to let go of the shit that she'd had pent up, to give her the release she'd really wanted. It seemed she just needed to cry, so I'd let her. She'd felt good in my arms, so soft and warm. I'd breathed in her scent. Strawberries. Fucking strawberries made me lose my mind.

She'd screwed with more than just my usual warm up routine because when I moved on to spar in the ring, the first round hadn't gone well. I had zero focus, and my opponent took advantage of that. My left knee was reaped and swelling because I'd let him take me to the mat. After a verbal beat down by Gray, I got my head in the game and put the sound of Harper coming out of my mind until I got to my shower, stroked my dick and came hard from the memory of her breathy moan, the way the scent of her pussy had lingered on my thumb.

I gave her two days to avoid me. Gave her the room to

process her emotions because she went through a fuck ton of them in just a few minutes. I wasn't sure if she was embarrassed or mad. Sad or horny or all of the above.

If she hated my guts, that was fine. At least she wasn't fucking Larry the Loser in a stairwell.

But two days had passed, and I hadn't seen her. Nothing. I had to know she was okay. After knocking on her door and getting no response, I went to see Emory. She'd given me a funny look when I'd asked her for Harper's cell number but said nothing as she put it in my phone.

Back in my chair, I tried not to think of how right she'd felt in my lap. Maybe it was a stupid idea, but I wanted to talk with her. And more. I shouldn't. She was too good for me, too damn perfect, even with whatever shit she was dealing with. I couldn't give her anything. I had some money—I saved most of my portion of my winnings and was starting to get endorsements. Even if I did bring in the heavy purses and made bucket loads of cash, I'd still never fit into her country club lifestyle, the stuffy faculty meet-and-greets. I'd never be smart enough for her. I wasn't *enough* for her.

But that didn't stop my thumbs from moving awkwardly over the tiny keyboard on my phone. I'd never sent a text to a woman before. I'd never had to. More importantly, I'd never wanted to. I sighed, knowing it was a dumb move, but hit send anyway.

Me: I want you on my lap again.

I did. That was the fucking truth. I wasn't going to say romantic shit to her about flowers and rainbows, especially in a text. That wasn't me. But I also wasn't going to tell her what I wanted to do to her. *With* her. Watching her come

64

had stirred up all kinds of killer fantasies, and they all involved her in my bed.

After two hours of watching crappy TV and icing my knee, I gave up on getting a response and went to bed. Had I fucked things up by pushing her the other day? Had I scared her away with my damn text? I might have sounded like a fucking middle schooler, but those were the thoughts that kept me tossing and turning all night. Again.

When the alarm went off on my phone at the usual five-thirty, I wiped the sleepy grit from my eyes and saw she'd responded. Two hours earlier when I had the sound programmed off. What the hell was she doing up that late?

> Harper: Didn't I embarrass myself enough
> the first time?

I ran my hand over my face, felt the beard that was starting.

> Me: That wasn't what I remember about it.
> Go out with me.

I hit send and then realized what I'd done. I wasn't fully awake. Why the hell was I texting before the sun came up? To a woman? I just asked Harper out. On a date. I didn't *do* dates, I remembered, dropping my cell on my unmade bed and throwing on my workout clothes. I slipped sweats and a hoodie over top and grabbed my running shoes.

I waited for the elevator. Yeah, it was a lazy ass move instead of taking the stairs, but I was stalling my run and giving myself time to wait for her to respond back. My phone dinged as I stepped on, pressed the button for the ground floor. I glanced down at the screen.

Harper: Can't.

I stopped halfway out the elevator, and the doors bumped my shoulders, prodding me to move. Gray was waiting in the lobby, tying his running shoes. He was dressed for the bitter cold in sweatpants, an insulated jacket and a skull cap on his head.

Me: Can't or won't?

Harper: Can't. I'm in London.

I frowned. "Why the fuck is Harper in London?" I asked Gray, holding my phone out.

He looked up and raised an eyebrow as he stood. We didn't usually talk before we finished the first mile of our run.

"Work, I think," he replied.

That was why she hadn't responded the night before. England was what, seven hours ahead? She'd been asleep. I ran my thumbs over my screen.

Me: You running from me?

She hadn't mentioned a work trip, but then again, she hadn't mentioned much of anything about herself. I knew what she did for a living and knew she had the endurance of an ultra-marathoner. I was somewhat aware of a shitty family and her misplaced source of comfort in sex with faceless men. That wasn't much, and I had a feeling it all tied in together somehow. And the damn elevator. The woman was fucking complicated. I didn't *do* complicated, didn't even know how. But I did know I needed to figure her out. I needed to get her to feel safe with me, with not just her personal safety, but to let her guard down and give herself over to someone completely. To *me* completely.

Yeah, I was a hypocrite. I was a fighter, and it was my job to keep my guard up. I didn't let anyone in whether it was in the ring or not. I'd had a shitty childhood with really, really shitty parents. I had enough baggage of my own that I refused to share with anyone. Gray may have gotten big bits and pieces out of me over the years, but he didn't know it all. Didn't know how truly bad it had been. But Harper, she'd one-two punched me the first time I laid eyes on her, and I was still sucking wind. I just worried I always would.

Harper: I'm running from everything.

Shit.

Gray tucked his hat lower on his head and went outside, saw his breath form in a white cloud beneath the entry lights. I couldn't text Harper back. I wasn't a thirteen-year-old girl and didn't have the dexterity in my thumbs. Besides, Gray was waiting, and what was going on was too big for a fucking text. I slipped my cell into the band on my biceps, tugged on my running shoes and joined him outside, breathing in the biting air. Harper was something I was going to figure out. Later.

9

REED

"Who the fuck is that?" I asked, pointing out the window of the gym.

A car was in the lot, two men sitting in it. A black Cadillac, but it wasn't a limo. The wheels were pimped out, and it didn't have livery tags. They weren't coming to the gym, and they didn't look the type to buy flowers for their girlfriends from the florist next door.

Gray came over, crossed his arms over his chest. I grabbed my towel from a bench, wiped my sweaty face. My hands were taped, and my feet were bare. We were taking a break between rounds of sparring. Thor had come in directly from work, and we were waiting for him to get changed. I knew I was big, but Thor made me look like a gangly teenager. He could have played pro football, if he liked the sport. He took the BJJ class and sparred but skipped the more brutal aspects of MMA. His wife had enough of a leash on him to keep him from getting hurt.

"They're not here for memberships," Gray said.

I huffed out a laugh. From what I could see of them, they lifted more doughnuts and beers than weights.

"Mid-twenties, expensive shades," I observed. The sun was just about to set, and while bitterly cold out, the sun was bright. "Expensive car."

"Punk attitudes."

I agreed with Gray's assessment. There was something obvious and cocky about punks. They thought their shit didn't stink. In the ring, they thought they could take anyone down and talked enough smack for people to believe it. But their bad-ass attitude only lasted about thirty seconds when they tapped out then complained about an unfair fight. Whatever.

We both knew those assholes. They came into the gym on occasion, trying to prove they were better than Gray, me, all of his fighters. Like the doctor's kid from the other day. Gray gladly—and quickly—proved them wrong. They didn't linger. It wasn't that kind of gym.

"They could be from my past."

I stated it plainly, without emotion. I didn't bring it up, but it was a strong possibility. These guys were in the wrong part of town. Sometimes, I felt I was, too. My past was a fucking cesspool. I'd gotten out of the shittiest neighborhood in Denver and never looked back. I'd tried, put too much effort in doing so, but it seemed no matter how hard I tried to leave it all behind, sometimes it came to you. Like the two sitting in the Caddy looking across the parking lot. Had my past caught up to me? No one in any of the rundown houses on my block had the cash for a pimped-out ride like that back in the day.

Times had changed. Drugs and other shit had moved in. I'd gained some notoriety with my fighting but the good kind. No drugs, no booze, no wild partying. I fought clean, and I lived clean, and I wouldn't waste any hard-earned cash on a POS status car. I was fine with my POS pickup truck.

"You're not going back to that shit, so why would they be here now?" he asked.

My parents were dead. I'd cut all ties from my old neighborhood when I went to juvie, then I'd gone right into the army. I hadn't even gone back when I'd been discharged, just came directly to be Gray's fighter. I hadn't figured it out at the time, but juvie had been the best thing for me. Perhaps the judge had known that, that I'd get a second chance if I was pulled out of my old life and away from the people who'd been dragging me down. I'd have either sunk into drugs like my mother or doing fifteen for armed robbery like my dad before he'd died. Maybe I'd be dead now, too. Fuck, no maybe about it.

Here, I was away from the violence, the drugs, the drinking, the crime. The death. Hell, these days I rarely even ate carbs. I was like a Boy Scout in comparison to my teenage years.

"I have no fucking clue. I'll go and find out."

I tossed the used towel in a laundry basket next to the bench.

Gray's hand on my arm stopped me. "Let them be. Just keep an eye out, and we'll see what they do, who they're here for. I'll tell the others to watch as well."

The others were his regulars, guys he could count on to help out in the gym, who had his back. Who knew what to watch for when there was trouble.

"Why are they sitting there?" I wiped my face with my

hand. "If they're not here for me, you think those are Dominguez's men?"

Gray shrugged. "Wouldn't put it past him. I don't like this," he added after a minute. The men hadn't moved from the spot. They saw us but didn't give a shit. If they were here to intimidate an opponent, to make me shake with fear over the fight with Sammy, it wasn't working. Those two goons? I could take on both of them with one hand tied behind my back. I assumed Dominguez would know it, too. Maybe that was why they stayed outside.

"Intimidation, gambling, even talking shit is all part of the game. Coming to the gym like this... it's new, even for me," Gray added.

Yeah, I didn't like it either, but I could defend myself, in the ring and on the street. I doubted they were here waiting to jump me in the lot. If I was hurt, there was no fight. No purse. Injuring me did them no good.

"We watch the women," he said, turning away. I knew he was going to his office to call Emory. If she was out, he'd meet her in the lot, walk her inside when she got back. He'd said "women," meaning he wanted Harper watched, too.

For once, I was relieved she was in another country. Safe from danger that could be my fault.

10

$\mathcal{H}$ARPER

JET LAG WAS KILLING ME. It did every time, and I had yet to find a way to make it better. I barely made it through the last lectures of the term and the staff meetings, and that was before I left. Now in the UK, I turned down the polite offers of dinner to instead return to my hotel room to sleep. I came to England about three times a year and stayed at the same quaint place, met with the same professors in the art history department. It was familiar. The faces were familiar, and I considered many to be friends. Lately, London was a safe haven. I was an ocean away from Cam, from my life. I could take a break from it, compartmentalize it all in my head and let it go, knowing it was so far away.

I was safe in England. I *felt* safe, like I was a different person. I'd been coaxed and swayed several times toward taking a permanent teaching position at the university here, but I'd always turned them down. But now with Cam getting out of jail, with him pressuring me, perhaps it was time to go where he couldn't get me. Since it would be a parole violation, he wouldn't follow.

I'd be safe.

My mind spun, circling around and around. It was the middle of the night, and I was wide awake. The street lights filtered in through the break in the curtains of my hotel room, street sounds muffled by the thick windows. I was comfortable in the dark, cozy in the room with the slanted ceiling and exposed beams.

Yet I'd never felt more alone. I picked up my cell from the bedside table, checked the clock. Two-thirty. I'd come directly back from the last meeting, taken a shower and slept a solid eight hours. There was no chance I was going back to sleep. I found a text I'd missed earlier from Giles. Giles Armstrong-Smythe, the lecturer who specialized in Norman architecture. It was a few centuries before my area of expertise, but we were in the same department.

I saw his face in my mind, the dark hair, the aristocratic nose. Heard his clipped English accent. He was handsome and a few years older than me. He'd been married once, now divorced. I was the foreigner, the woman he could fuck and forget every time I flew home. I should have been bothered by the casualness of it all, but I liked it that way. He probably didn't realize just how much. It had only happened twice and both times in the musty storage closet next to his office in the Arts building. Only the required clothing had been removed to get the job done. Nothing more. I hadn't come either time, but I'd made the connection, soothed the loneliness I'd felt if only for a little bit. Eased the burden of remembering what had happened to me and the lack of support from my family.

Of course, he knew I was back for the meetings and

presentations and wanted more no-strings-attached action. Why wouldn't he? I offered him no-strings fucking. I wasn't clingy, I wasn't anything really to him. He wasn't anything to me.

The vision of him transformed to Reed. His dark hair. His ice blue eyes. The way his lip kicked up at the corner when amused. The heated anger at seeing me with Larry. His voice when he'd coaxed me to come from just the motion of his thumb. He'd texted me while I was in a morning meeting. I got hot all over just thinking about the words.

Reed: I want you on my lap again.

God, that sounded really, really appealing, yet it scared the shit out of me. While I'd allowed men like Giles to touch me, to fuck me, they hadn't seen me. I didn't bare my body or my soul to any of them. They knew nothing about me, saw nothing past their own arousal and desires. To get off. And I wanted it that way. I didn't want anyone to see my flaws, everything dirty in my past. In my life.

With Reed, when I'd been on his lap, I'd been completely covered, he'd touched me over my panties, and I'd never been so exposed. Vulnerable. *He* hadn't gotten off. He hadn't even gotten a kiss.

Still, he *saw* me. Saw into me, into the deep places I kept hidden, that I traveled five thousand miles to escape. In his texts, he'd asked me if I was running from him, and I'd answered him honestly. Distance helped with telling the truth. I *was* running from everything, and it had been the first time I'd admitted it, even to myself.

I was running from my life, and just like on the treadmill

at the gym, I wasn't going anywhere. I was stuck. Trapped. Not just by Cam but by my own doing.

I did the math. Bit my lip. Two-thirty here, seven-thirty in Colorado. Reed had left the conversation open, asking me out, which meant he wanted to know more about me. I wanted that, I did, but then he might see the cracks in my facade. He might see the truth, and then he'd be gone. Who would want to stay with someone like me?

I got up, got a drink of water from the sink in the bathroom. Stared at myself in the old mirror over the narrow sink. Was I going to live like this? Meet Giles after the morning presentation for a quick fuck just so I felt better? Would I feel better? It used to work, but I didn't think it would now. Thinking of dropping to my knees before Giles made me nauseated. Ashamed.

What was wrong with me? I closed my eyes, sighed. God, I had been letting a stranger stick his dick in me for some twisted validation.

No. Reed was right. No more. I looked down at my cell, resting on the lip of the sink. I just had to push his name on my screen.

Engage. Connect. Then I wouldn't be alone.

I picked up the phone, pressed the little phone icon next to his name.

"Harper."

Just his voice had my heart beating frantically.

"Reed," I said. My voice was breathless. "I, um... sorry, did I catch you at the gym?"

"It's the middle of the night there. Are you okay?"

I exhaled, relaxed, at least a little bit. "Jet lag."

"I didn't know you were going away." No, I hadn't told him although we hadn't done much talking. "Work?"

I turned off the light in the bathroom and climbed onto

the bed, stacking the pillows against the mahogany headboard with my free hand, so I could sit up.

"I'm a guest lecturer at the university here, which has me doing joint research, leading seminars. This trip, there's a group presentation on the latest dig at the cathedral ruins at —" I sighed, realizing I sounded like an idiot. "Never mind. It's about a pile of really old rocks."

I heard him huff out a little laugh. "I don't need to know the complicated details. I just like hearing the excitement in your voice."

For a second, I had no idea how to respond.

"You like what you do," he continued.

"Yes," I replied, tucking my bare legs under the thick blankets. I was only in an old t-shirt and panties, and it was chilly, the space heated by an old radiator beneath the window. The cozy bedding and flannel sheets made up the difference.

"I can hear it when you talk about it. I thought you had finals here."

"I did, but they finished the other day. My TA closed out the grades."

"Aren't classes done for the holiday there, too?"

"Their term finished today."

"You'll be coming back to spend Christmas with your family?"

"Soon."

I wasn't going to offer him more, that I would spend the holiday alone. Telling him about why I would be by myself wasn't something I wanted to do, and I didn't want his pity. Byzantine art and a dysfunctional family were not topics any woman should share with a guy unless she wanted to drive him away.

He was quiet for a minute, but I didn't mind. "So, you

did run away."

I leaned back, slid lower into the pillows. "Yes."

"From me?" he asked, and I remembered his text earlier.

"You? No." I bit my lip. Took a chance. "From what you made me feel? Definitely."

"You don't like coming so hard you cry out?"

I felt my cheeks heat, and I groaned with embarrassment.

"Reed," I said, pleading with him to stop with just his name.

"That's not how you said it the other night."

I couldn't help but laugh. "You're terrible."

I heard him laugh, too. "I figured you'd say I was really, really good."

"You're really sure of yourself."

"I bet I could make you do it again."

I slid further down in bed, rubbed my thighs together. My pussy ached because he was right. Because I remembered how good it felt when he'd touched me. I had no doubt he could do it again. "Too bad I'm so far away," I replied.

"Princess, you doubt my skill?" I remained quiet. "Are you in bed?"

"Yes."

I heard his groan through the phone. "What are you wearing?"

"Reed," I said again, slightly stunned but mostly aroused. How could just his voice from thousands of miles away make me feel needy? "I'm not telling you that."

"You sleep naked, don't you?"

I huffed out a small laugh. "I am *not* answering that."

"That means yes. Christ, I'm hard just thinking about it."

And that made me wet. Knowing I turned him on made

me feel good. Good in a way I hadn't in a long time. But I wasn't ready for this, for him. He'd overwhelmed me the other night. He was overwhelming me now with just his... niceness. "I'm not having phone sex with you."

"Okay." His one word was even, calm.

I stilled, realizing he wasn't pushing, wasn't making me do something I didn't want to do. Well, I did want to do it. I wanted to do it really, really badly, but it was just as clinical as it would have been fucking Larry.

Still, he took my no as just that. No.

"But princess, remember what I said before. If you need to come, I'll give it to you. Even from far away. Don't go seeing the Englishman you have over there."

I stiffened, my fingers gripping the phone. "I don't know what you're—"

"Harper. I don't give a shit what you've done in the past, hell, *who* you've done in the past. Do I wish no one's had their hands on you before? Of course. But I won't be an asshole when I've got a past, too. I don't let that matter, and I won't let what you've done matter either. But I'll give you what you need now and keep you safe doing it."

He could see too much. He couldn't really know about Giles—he hadn't even known I was out of the country—but he'd seen me with Larry. Knew what I was going to do with him, how it hadn't meant anything, just a chance for me to forget for a few minutes. Reed had seen it in the stairwell, knew I'd probably have someone here in the UK, too. I didn't want to tell him he was right. I wasn't ready for it, even though I'd broken down on his lap. Gave me a release, in a way almost better than an orgasm.

I didn't know how to respond without revealing any more of me, so I ended the call without saying anything at all.

11

EED

AFTER TOSSING the cell onto the passenger seat, I closed my eyes, wrapped my fingers around the steering wheel. I was parked across the street from where I grew up in the shitty part of town. The house was gutted. The windows had been shattered on the second floor, the lower ones covered in warped wood with graffiti sprayed on it. The brick facade was chipped and starting to collapse. It was too dark to see the smoke damage, but I knew it was there. The houses on either side were vacant and abandoned, too. Hell, almost every one on the street gutted.

All was quiet, but that was deceiving. Steam rose from the manhole covers, proving it was too cold to be outside, even for the rats that usually darted out to find food. Not that anyone smart would be walking the streets in this part of town after the sun went down. It wasn't a safe place. No, it was rough like me. One had to be ready for anything here. Rough and ready, that was me. Old cars lined both sides of the road, the street lamp was blown out in the center of the block, and I had to wonder if it was a new development or if the city crew refused to come here to replace it.

This block was my past. My fucked-up childhood. Rough streets, rougher home life. In my mind, I saw my father's angry face, heard his vicious words, felt the hot sear of his belt. There was no forgetting my mother's drunk gaze as she let it all happen. The gym was an hour from here, but it could have been a world away. It was my life now, yet this shithole still close enough where it could easily come back to haunt me. I didn't want to be back, but I couldn't shake the two men who'd camped out in the gym's lot. They'd done nothing, just sat there and watched us then eventually left. One minute they were there, the next time I turned around, gone.

It couldn't be just a one-time thing. Not a chance in fucking hell.

Gray had shit with his dad. Old shit. I'd never met the man, but I knew he called Gray out of nowhere just to fuck with him. The asshole had him watched. Followed. He bet against his fights. And that was all since Gray returned from his army deployments. What happened when he was a kid... he didn't speak about it any more than I shared my own past, but it had been fucked up.

But after last summer's deal with Emory and the drug dealer who'd gone after her, the man had left Gray alone. Supposedly, Quake Baker had something on the dad, enough to make the bastard afraid. Afraid enough to leave his son alone. It helped that the older man was president of the No Holds Barred MC. I couldn't see Gray's dad stirring shit up now out of the blue. That left me. The men in the car had to have been there for me. But why?

My dad was dead. I'd seen to that. My mother had died a few years ago, her liver finally giving out on her in some women's shelter. The crowd I'd run with back in the day weren't part of a gang, at least they hadn't been years ago. The men in the car? Not gang members.

This place was tainted. *I* was tainted, and I'd taken Harper's call from here, staring out and seeing my past. When her name lit up my cell, I felt... happiness. Happiness in this hell hole. It only made me see all of the differences between us. Privilege and poverty. Brains and brawn.

I wanted Harper. Fuck, any man alive would see her long legs and wish they were wrapped around his waist. It was more than that. I wanted to hear her voice, see her smile. Make her fucking happy.

I'd told her I wasn't looking for a relationship. I hadn't been, never considered myself more than an easy lay for a woman who wanted a good time. Now, that held no appeal. No woman interested me but Harper. Somehow having her far away, unattainable, made me change my thinking. I may not have been looking for one, but a relationship had found me. I wasn't walking away from Harper or her shit ton of problems. I'd take them from her, make them mine. They couldn't be worse than anything I'd seen or lived through. I could handle it. Did that make me whipped? Fuck, yes. I had no idea how it happened or why I'd changed my thinking so damn quickly, but I wanted *more* from Harper.

A car passed, a cigarette flung out the window, the red glow of the tip the only color on the street. Harper deserved more than this. She deserved a guy from the country club who wore golf shirts and played squash on the weekends. A lawyer or some other high paying, career-driven man who could give her the lifestyle she was accustomed to.

This? Me? A fighter from the other side of the tracks who had a record and earned his salary with his fists? As I glanced one last time out the window before driving off, I had to wonder, would I ruin her?

12

*H*ARPER

Cam: Where are you?

MY BROTHER'S text ruined my morning. His three words had me distracted, and I offered nothing to the meeting I was in. When my colleagues had turned to me for a response, I'd offered a fake smile and blamed my lack of focus on jet lag. I had slept after I'd talked with Reed, surprisingly, but morning had come too quickly. The three cups of coffee I'd had did nothing to make me alert. But one text from Cam had my mind spinning, my heart pounding. Even if I put my head down on the table, I wouldn't have been able to sleep.

I refused to respond. There was no need. Cam didn't know where I was, couldn't touch me.

Cam: Your apartment is dark.

I clenched my phone when the second text came through a few hours later. We'd just returned from lunch at the nearby pub. I stood in the hallway, staring down at the words. My heart pounded so hard, it hurt. My lunch was debating whether to come back up. Cam was still in jail. I would've heard if he'd been released early. My mother would have called, cajoled once again in coming to her stupid party.

No, he was still in jail. Until tomorrow.

Then how did he know about my apartment? If he wasn't watching it, then someone else was. Had he hired someone on the outside to spy on me? Was someone else looking for me and pestering my brother? I wouldn't put it past the men he owed money to, and I wouldn't put it past my brother to offer me up again. But why had I been safe before now? It had been almost two years. I shivered, cold even in my cashmere turtleneck.

"I'm surprised you're here after term."

I startled at the voice. I turned on my heel and looked up at Giles. Yes, he was handsome, his dark hair falling rakishly over his forehead, and the slight twist of his lips when he smiled was appealing. He wore a tweed coat with the patches on the elbows along with hunter green wool pants. I wasn't sure if he fit the stereotype of an overly intelligent Englishman or a senior lecturer of arts. I thought back to when I'd gone to pick up pizza with Reed. He'd mentioned the elbow patches then and had been pretty accurate with his image of an art history professor.

I shrugged and tried to shake off Cam's text, but it was really hard. He had someone watching for me, and the thought that my apartment was no longer safe completely freaked me out.

I realized Giles was waiting for me to say something. I

pasted on a brittle smile. "This presentation is important to the department. I might only be a guest lecturer, but I like to help."

His lips turned, but his gaze drifted down my body before looking me in the eye.

"You could be more than just a guest. You could take the job I know you've been offered."

I could and based on Cam's latest text, the idea held more and more appeal.

"Everyone's going home after the presentation for the long holiday. Are you headed to the airport—" He stepped close, close enough that anyone passing would think we were more than just colleagues. "—or are you staying for a few days?"

A few days meant time in his bed. Not just the storage closet down the hall. God, it would be so easy to take what he offered, giving myself to someone, to forget Cam and my fucked-up life. Giles was harmless. He wouldn't hurt me. Sleeping with him would give me just what I ached for. Arms to hold me as I struggled. A sated man to know I had something to offer. The attraction between us had been enough where I'd been wet when we fucked, but not enough to come. That hadn't been his fault. No one made me come. And no one took me to his bed.

I thought of Reed. His bad boy looks that didn't match the way he touched me. The way he hadn't taken anything from me. The way *he'd* made me come. *He* was the only one to have done so.

Giles' fingers squeezed my shoulder, bringing me out of my thoughts. His touch was gentle but didn't awaken me as he probably wanted. As he once had. I breathed in his crisp cologne and missed Reed's clean scent: soap, sweat and man.

"I'm... I'm not sure yet."

I lied. I was staying. My return ticket was for Christmas day, but I didn't know if I wanted to spend any of the time before then with him. I craved the thought of him touching me, of the connection I'd feel when he was inside me. I hurt, and I knew I'd be soothed, even if temporarily. I craved the *thought*. Not him.

"Or." He drew the word out, so I had to meet his gaze. Only then did he lean in, whisper, "Or we could go to one of the study rooms down the hall. They're empty since the term is over."

My gaze flicked to the side corridor where there were a row of small rooms used as quiet work spaces. The building was Victorian with wood paneling and stone floors and laid out with the mindset of an 1800's architect. The only people in the building were the lecturers and guests involved in the meeting. There were a number of places where we could go for a quickie without being seen or heard. Before I could respond, someone waved to us from down the hall, prompting our return to work. Giles sighed at the opportunity lost. Not that I was going to agree, but I had before.

I entered the meeting room, Giles having opened the door for me. I didn't miss the look he gave me. We weren't done talking. I took my seat, and the discussion about the proposed foundation work picked up, but I looked down at the phone in my lap, at Cam's latest text. I felt the anger, the frustration build again.

This was the moment Reed was talking about. The moment when I wanted to grab Giles and drag him into a study room and fuck. I wouldn't get off, I would only see the smile of satisfaction on his face as he tied off the used condom and tossed it in the trash. I'd feel good knowing I made him feel good, but that was it. There was nothing in it for me. No satisfaction. I'd have to wait until I was back in my hotel room to touch myself, to make myself come. Then, it would be an empty release. But I'd forget about Cam, about how he was going to be free tomorrow. If he could mess with me from jail, I could only imagine what he was going to do when he got out. Then there were my parents. He'd already pitted them against me.

I let my eyes slip closed, aching for a connection, knowing I was pathetic. I used sex as a way to validate my worth, and it wasn't working. It only made it worse. A painful lump lodged in my throat. Tears. I wasn't a crier. No. I didn't cry. I *wouldn't* cry here. Not in a roomful of people. Colleagues.

With shaking fingers, I typed out a text to Reed.

Me: Awake?

I lifted my head, listened to the woman at the far end of the table speaking about English historic preservation laws until I felt my cell vibrate in my palm.

Reed: Good thing you're not a math professor.
Your time zone calculations are terrible.
It's 9. Just finished my morning training.

The corner of my mouth tipped up and somehow, I felt better. Just knowing Reed was there, even from so far away. I'd reached out, and he'd responded. I could see him in those MMA shorts he wore, the black ones that rode low on his lean hips, the ones with the little slits on the sides of the thighs. I couldn't miss the hard muscle there whenever he moved. He'd be wearing a T-shirt, damp with his sweat, his dark hair a mess, scruff on his jaw. I squirmed in my hard chair at the vision in my head.

> Reed: How are the fish and chips? See the
> Loch Ness Monster?

I bit my lip to keep from smiling outright.

> Me: Boring meeting.
> Reed: That's the problem with being so
> smart. You have to use your brain. I get to
> work with my fists.

I thought about those hands and what he'd been able to do with them. The way they'd touched me so gently even knowing how dangerous they could be.

> Me: I'm not paying any attention to the
> meeting.
> Reed: Are you being a bad girl, princess?

I bit back a laugh.

> Me: Me?
> Reed: You can be whatever you want with me.
> Me: I don't think I know how. To be bad, I
> mean.

Reed didn't respond right away, and I panicked I'd said the wrong thing. I felt exposed and vulnerable even though Reed wasn't even in the same country. What was he thinking? I saw Giles look my way, and I straightened, pretending to listen to the rules on modern encroachment and setbacks. I studied the past, the art and the buildings. While it was important to maintain what was so dear to me, the English legalese was something I could easily tune out.

> Reed: Excuse yourself from the meeting and
>   go to the ladies room.

I glanced up, looked at the eight other people in the room, all intently listening to the discussion.

> Me: What?
> Reed: You're a PhD. I know you can read. Go.

I sat there for a moment, stunned. Should I do as Reed said? Why did he want me to go to the ladies' room? I took a moment, realized no one knew about my conversation. A wicked thrill shot through me. Reed made me curious, made me feel a little wicked.

I pushed back my chair and stood, quietly excusing myself. I went out into the hall and passed the nearest ladies' room and entered the one at the far end of the hall.

> Me: OK

When the phone vibrated again, it wasn't to signal another text, but a call from Reed. I fumbled to answer, then lifted it to my ear. "Hi."

"What's the matter?"

I leaned against the wall. "What do you mean?"

The bathroom hadn't been modernized in decades, the sink and stalls straight from the fifties. The ancient radiator pumped out heat and made the small space dry and stuffy.

"I know you didn't text to tell me you're saying yes to my offer for dinner. What's going on, princess?"

"Why do you call me that?"

"Because in comparison to me, you're a princess."

"You don't know anything about me."

Yeah, I grew up with money, but that was it. I wasn't spoiled. I certainly wasn't coddled or protected.

"Then tell me something." His words were even, as if he hadn't heard the defensive tone in my reply.

I sighed. "What do you want to know?"

"Everything."

I didn't reply. Was he joking?

"I mean it."

"Why?" I turned sideways and pressed my shoulder against the wall as I held the phone to my ear.

"Why?" he repeated.

"Why do you want to know everything about me?"

He sighed. "I have no fucking idea. I just do. I want to know what's inside your head."

I laughed then, the sound echoing. "You already do."

"I do?" The question had a serious tone to it.

"God, you made me cry. I'm not telling you that to make you feel bad, but I haven't cried in two years."

"Why not?"

"Because there weren't any tears left."

Shit. I'd said a lot, perhaps too much. When he didn't say anything, I said his name to fill the void. "You need to tell me something about yourself now. It's only fair."

"All right. Let me think." He was quiet for a few seconds, and I heard the crackle of the line. "My first time, I was fourteen."

I couldn't imagine him as a scrawny, gangly kid.

"She was older, sixteen. Amanda Carter. I was too

nervous, too worked up to put the condom on, so she helped me. I, well—" I could hear the chagrin in his voice. "—let's just say I didn't last."

"You didn't—"

"Three times. I pumped into her three times, and I came. I think it was all of twelve seconds."

I put my hand over my face, felt my smile.

"I'm afraid, princess, that when I finally sink into you, I won't even last that long."

My mouth fell open. "You mean you have a problem?"

He chuckled. "No, it means you have me so hot I'm probably going to make a fool of myself."

I had absolutely no idea what to say to that.

"What about you?" he asked.

"Me?"

"Your first time."

I was still stuck on his confident statement that we were going to have sex. "Oh, um, my brother's friend."

"How old were you?"

"Thirteen."

I thought I heard him swear, but it was barely a whisper. "How old was he?"

"Eighteen."

"Were you dating or going out or whatever they called it in your prep school world?"

"Oh, um. No. Cam—my brother—and his friend were watching movies, and they came into the kitchen where I was studying. They invited me to join them, so I did. Then halfway through the movie, Cam told me to go with Brad for a little fun."

"Go where?" Reed's voice was darker, almost black.

"To my brother's room. It wasn't too bad. I heard it hurts

for every girl the first time. He was... nice. I heard he died a few years later. Car accident."

I heard a thud, perhaps a door closing. "Princess, that's um, I think I need to have a little talk with your brother."

I turned to the wall, leaned my forehead against it. Picked at a flake in the cream paint. "You can't. He's in prison." Realizing I said too much, I backtracked. "You're not interested in all that. Look, I should probably get back to the meeting."

"Right."

I didn't want to end the call, but I didn't want to talk about my past either. My life was what it was. It wasn't going to change, especially my past. "Thanks, Reed."

"For what?"

"Being there."

13

EED

I was glad Harper was so far away. If she saw me now, she'd be afraid. I'd been so angry when she told me what had happened to her, I heel palmed the cinderblock wall. The throbbing pain dulled my need to beat the shit out of her brother, and I shook my wrist to work it out. I knew better than to injure myself, but fuck, this woman pulled out every one of my protective instincts. I'd been born to fight. Hell, I'd survived by fighting, and I wouldn't hesitate to defend someone I cared about.

Did I care about Harper? Fuck, yes.

Why? I had no idea. I just knew the second I saw her she was different.

More.

When I'd seen her text, I'd just finished my workout and was heading upstairs to shower. Sweat dripped down my face, made my t-shirt cling. I was ripe and ready for a protein shake and my usual lunch of salmon and brown rice.

I'd walked out of the gym and into the emergency stairs leading to our apartments, sat down on the hard steps as we talked, but when she'd shared about what her brother had done, *given* her to his friend, I couldn't hold back. I'd had to hit something. I wanted to hit the fucker Brad. Good thing he was dead. No, I wanted to hit her brother more. An older brother was supposed to watch out for a sister, not *give* her to a friend. Fuck!

I'd had to keep my cool, to hide the rage that seeped from me like the sweat from my morning training session. Harper had done nothing wrong, and she didn't need to feel bad about what had happened to her. She'd been practically a child. Thirteen! What the hell did she know about sex at thirteen? From the sound of it, she played it off as something that wasn't rape. It hadn't sounded like the guy forced her, but what kind of consent could she give? She might not have said no, but I doubted she'd been into it, that she'd said yes. She'd been *thirteen.*

Jesus.

Maybe that was how she coped although knowing she'd been ready to fuck Larry in this damn stairwell meant she wasn't completely straightened out. She'd left the country. Fled to London. Maybe what we'd done in my apartment had set her off, but I was sure it wasn't the only reason she'd run. Something else was going on. She'd texted me though —and not because she was bored. Although if I had to sit through a meeting about a seven-hundred-year-old cathedral, I'd lose my mind. No, she didn't know anything about me except that I was safe. That I'd listen, hold her, protect her.

Since she'd just let slip that her brother gave her to his

friend, it was a sign that she trusted me, at least a little but, in a way she'd never expected. Our friendship, whatever the fuck it was, was unexpected. The princess and the guy on the wrong side of the tracks. Somehow, I could give her things no one else could. I wasn't exactly sure what that was since I had no idea what the fuck I was doing. When it came to women, I didn't do relationships. I didn't do anything deep because I didn't want anyone to see past the fighter veneer because no one would like what they found.

I just knew I had to be there for her. The rest, I'd figure out.

I went back into the gym, tracked down Gray, who was with a client by the punching bags warming up. The guy, Wiley, was debating going pro. He was good, and if anyone was going to get him there, it was Gray. Wiley was kicking the crap out of the bag, one after the other, the dense sound of it louder than the music through the overhead speakers.

"Good, now roll your hip over. Yes, like that. Again."

Gray kept his eyes on his client but gave a little chin lift, a sign I could interrupt.

I stepped close, murmured, "Who's the cop who comes to the BJJ class?"

Gray arched one dark brow, crossed his arms over his chest. He wore a gym T-shirt and his black grappling shorts. His feet were bare since he was on the mats. "Jasper?"

I nodded. "That's him. I need him to find out about someone."

"Go grab a drink, grab your gloves, and I'll meet you in the ring," Gray said to Wiley.

Wiley said hi to me on the way to the bench where he grabbed his towel, mopped the sweat from his face as he grabbed his water bottle.

Gray and I stood alone in the far side of the gym. "Someone?"

"Harper's brother. Said his name was Cam, and he's in prison."

"From your tone, it sounds bad."

I met his steel colored eyes. "Real bad."

"Then let's keep it from the cops. I'll call Quake Baker."

The man had taken Emory under his protection. He ran a diner on the far side of town, a business legitimate, but I had no doubt he dabbled in less legal endeavors as president of a motorcycle club. I wasn't going to ask about them, but I'd learned from Gray he'd taken care of the asshole who'd broken into Emory's house. Quake was a good ally to have, especially with situations like this. He had the same thoughts as me and Gray—no one fucked with anyone's woman.

"Good."

"Want back in the ring?" he asked as we walked toward Wiley.

I glanced to Gray, grinned. My roiling anger was obvious, and there was one way to burn some of it off. With my fists, just as I wanted. Wiley would be good competition. "Definitely."

14

$\mathcal{H}$ARPER

Reed: Do you like Thai food?

Me: Yes. Why?

Reed: I want to know what you like for when we go out.

Me: I never said yes.

Reed: Say yes.

Me: To Thai food?

Reed: To me.

Me: About what?

Reed: I told you before. Everything.

Me: I told you no to phone sex.

Reed: OK. How about texting sex?

Me: I have no idea how to do that.

Reed: What are you wearing?

Me: It's midnight.

Reed: I didn't ask what time it was.

Me: A T-shirt and underwear.

Reed: Underwear? Like boxers?

Me: Panties. Like lace.

Reed: Shit. Slip your hand inside those hot-as-fuck lace panties and play with your clit.

Me: I can't do this.

Reed: What? Come? You came for me before.

Me: No, I can't do texting sex.

Reed: Why not? It's more fun than I thought. Touch yourself, princess.

Me: Is it all one-sided with you?

Reed: Sex?

Me: Yes.

Reed: Princess, I have my hand on my dick and pre-cum is dripping from it like a faucet. This is not one sided.

OH MY GOD. I was in bed reading. I pushed myself up and leaned against the headboard and stared at the texts. Reed may have gotten me off in his lap, and I knew he was into me, but he'd never actually said anything so... sexual to me before. I was imagining Reed sitting in his recliner with his hands down his workout shorts. I imagined him big, thick. Perfect.

Reed: Princess? Did I scare you away?

I blinked then panicked that he worried I was freaking out.

Me: No. I was... thinking about what you said.

Reed: Me rubbing one out while thinking
    of you?
Me: Yes.
Reed: I want you to come with me. Over your
    panties like before if you want.

I wanted. God, did I want. I was five thousand miles away from Reed. He couldn't see me. He couldn't hear me. He wouldn't judge. I didn't think, just dropped the cell on the bed and tugged off my T-shirt, then pushed my undies down my legs and tossed them onto the floor. I settled back into the bed, parted my legs.

Me: OK
Reed: Sorry, I dropped the phone. Fuck, ok.

I smiled and felt... silly. Light. As if I were sharing something secret. This was one of the most intimate things I'd ever done with someone, and yet he wasn't even here. I began to touch myself in the way I knew would get me off. I didn't play, just put my three fingers together and rubbed in circles just the right way. My feet slid up, and my knees spread. I cried out into the empty hotel room as I came, harder than I could ever remember. I was sweaty and breathing hard and... happy. I slapped my hand down on the bed searching for the cell, grabbed it up.

Me: Ok
Reed: You came?
Me: Yes
Reed: Shit... kde*d. S ksdfs we2

I stared and tried to figure out what he was saying.

99

> Reed: Fuck, sorry. Can't type one handed and
> can't type shit when I'm coming all over
> my hand.
> Me: Oh

I flushed thinking about him. He'd come because of me. *Thinking* of me. I'd made him that way. It was powerful. Exhilarating.

> Reed: Go to sleep, princess. You need me, I'm
> here.

———

REED

"THEY'RE BACK." Gray stood before the wall of windows that overlooked the parking lot. His arms were crossed, his gaze serious. He was always serious. The only person I knew who could make him smile was Emory.

I moved to stand beside him, my jump rope hanging from my fingers.

"Shit."

The sky was leaden, the air almost foggy, which meant it was cold as shit out. Flurries were starting to fall. By morning, there would be a few inches of it on the ground. The gym was warm, and I was sweating from my workout. "I think it's time to go say hi."

Gray looked to me. Nodded.

We walked out the doors to the lot, the cold air hitting me, my skin instantly drying. My T-shirt would be frozen if I lingered. I wasn't planning on it.

I walked over to the driver's window as Gray stood in front of the car. The man rolled down the window as I approached, hot air and the smell of cigarettes hitting me.

"Tell Dominguez hello for me."

The punk was in his thirties, a thick, black cap on his head, the Broncos logo on the front. He was white and pasty, had greasy hair and when he grinned at me, a gold tooth.

"Who the fuck is Dominguez?" he asked. "If you're looking to score, you're at the wrong car."

I slowly shook my head. "You want to play it like that?" I rolled my shoulders, and the guy's smile slipped.

The one in the passenger seat, at least fifty pounds overweight and looking like Jabba the Hut with his bald, sweaty head, piped up. "Dude, we don't want anything to do with you."

I glanced to Gray. "Oh yeah? Why's that? I'm the one that's fighting."

"Fighting? What the fuck are you talking about?"

I frowned. "Why the fuck are you here?" I asked back, kicking back the belligerent tone.

"Not for you, asshole." He glanced up at the building, then back at me.

I looked to Gray again. This time he wasn't just an observer. He came around to stand beside me. "You even think about my girl, and they won't know where to find your body."

After the shit that went down with Emory over the summer, Gray was protective as hell. No one would fuck with her. The last guy? I wasn't exactly sure what happened to him, but I knew Quake Baker got involved. If an MC dealt with him, then he was dead and buried where no one could find. Still, Gray wasn't going to let down his guard.

The driver, hell, both of them held up their hands in

surrender. "We know who the fuck you are. You think we'd fuck with The Outlaw? We want nothing to do with your girl."

"Then who?" Gray asked, his voice as cold and icy as the air.

"Dude, we're outta here." Jabba the Hut smacked his friend's arm, and he took the hint. He put the car in gear and backed out fast enough to make the wheels squeal on the pavement.

"Catch the license plate?" he asked.

I nodded, watching the shitty sedan cut into traffic.

"They're not here for Emory," I said, keeping my eyes on the street, even though they were long gone. If they weren't here for her, then why were they—

"No. But I'll be more careful just the same. Might be time to call a friend."

I figured the *friend* was Quake, and that was fine with me. That guy could get the details on the plate easier than going to the cops. Hell, the cops wouldn't give us anything, but Quake would.

Those assholes were thugs, pure and simple. They scared people, shook them for money, made threats. I wasn't scared of them. Neither was Gray. We just had to figure out what the fuck they wanted. Those two shits weren't the boss. No way. They took orders. But who gave them and why?

15

EED

Harper: You'll be proud of me.

I SAW THE TEXT, and I grinned. The bar was crowded, the music so loud I felt it vibrate through the floor. I had no interest in the scene. I wasn't drinking since I was training, and I wasn't looking for pussy like the others were. I felt like an old man with the other fighters I was with. One was dancing with a curvy blonde, his hand riding low on her waist as she all but humped his thigh. Yeah, I wouldn't be giving him a ride home tonight. Two others were seated beside me at a high top, but they were turned toward the dance floor, scoping out the women.

After the evening BJJ class, I was pulled into going to a bar and watching the fights, checking out the competition, then we'd gone onto another bar, then this one. It was late, after two. I felt like an old man, not used to the late hour.

Shit, I was usually asleep by ten. Late night partying didn't work with pre-dawn workouts.

I'd felt my phone vibrate in my pocket, and when I saw Harper's text, I spun around, facing away from everyone.

> Me: Oh yeah?
> Harper: You're awake. Thought you'd see this
>   when you got up.
> Me: No worries, princess. Why am I proud
>   of you?
> Harper: Some of my colleagues were talking
>   about MMA, and I was able to keep up. I
>   spoke their language.
> Me: I thought they spoke English over there.
> Harper: I meant MMA talk. I knew what an
>   RNC is.

I laughed then, picturing her making the arm motions for the rear naked choke, one of the many submissions in the sport.

> Me: And how do you know about all that?
> Harper: I watched you on YouTube.
> Me: Ten minutes. Call me.
> Harper: Oh. I'm sorry. I didn't realize you
>   were with someone. Sorry.
> Me: Don't be sorry. And I'm with the guys not
>   someone. Call me in ten minutes,
>   princess.

I stood then patted one of my friends on the shoulder and signaled I was leaving. I gave them both hand slaps—it was too loud to talk—and I bolted.

My apartment door closed behind me as my phone rang. "Hey."

"Hey."

"I'm sorry to bother when you're with--"

"Princess," I said with a whole lot of frustration.

She sighed, and I heard it across the miles. "What are we doing?" she asked.

I toed off my shoes, shrugged out of my coat as I pressed my phone to my ear with my shoulder.

"Talking."

I heard her sigh. "This is way more than talking."

I had no intention of telling her about the guys in the parking lot. If they weren't for her, it didn't matter. If they were there for her, I didn't want to freak her out when she was so far away. I wanted her to freak out with me right beside her.

"Want to have phone sex?" I asked, trying again although not overly serious. One of these days, I'd get her relaxed enough with me to say yes.

She paused. "No."

I stilled just inside my bedroom doorway. "Do you mean that no?"

Another pause. "No. You said... you said I shouldn't get off with some random guy."

Her voice lacked the usual determination. I ran my hand through my hair, frustrated that she still didn't get it. Fuck, someone did a number on her. I had to assume it was her brother or *at least* her brother to start. "I'm not a random guy, princess. We sexted last night. And, I said if you need to get off, I'm the one to help."

She was quiet, and I didn't fill the silence. I waited her out. "I thought about it," she finally admitted. "With someone else, I mean. Considered it earlier. It was offered."

I flicked on my bedside lamp, a soft glow filled the room.

Anger bubbled up. Sexting didn't mean commitment, but she'd considered fucking an Englishman after what we'd done? "A random guy wanted a quick fuck with you?"

"Not so random but yes."

"What did you decide?"

We weren't anything. She could fuck anyone she wanted, and I had no right to get mad. It didn't mean I had to like the idea. I didn't even know the guy, and I wanted to beat the shit out of him because he held no value for her if all he wanted was a willing hole for his dick.

"And?" I asked, holding my breath.

"And I turned him down."

Thank fuck. "Because..."

She was quiet for a bit. "Because sexting with you is better than a quick fuck with him."

I couldn't help but sigh as I dropped onto my bed. "Then you need to get off again?"

"You want me to hang up, so we can sex text?"

"Hell, no," I countered. "I want to hear you." Fuck, did I want to listen to the sound she made when she came.

I waited, the crackle of the line almost deafening as I did so.

"It feels impersonal," she admitted.

"What? Phone sex? As compared to sexting? Or Larry?" It was harsh, but I wanted to know. Needed to know her mind on this.

"Maybe more so than if I'd fucked Larry."

I growled, and I didn't give a shit if she heard it. "This, between us, princess? It's nothing like what you would've done with Larry or that English prick who wanted to use you to blow his load. What we share, it's special. Sexting or whatever we do. I want to ask you to take off your clothes, to stand in front of your hotel mirror and look at your gorgeous body. I want you to describe to me what you're seeing. The color of your nipples, the way they harden. I want you to tell me how wet you are, if your thighs are coated with your need. I want to hear how swollen your clit is then hear the moan you make when you touch it."

She whimpered.

"All that?" I said, running a hand over my face. "It's not impersonal because all the while, you're going to wish it was my hands on you, my mouth."

"This... this is special?"

Out of everything I said, that was what she asked after. "Fuck, princess." I gripped my shirt at the back of my neck, tugged it over my head, let it drop to the floor. I leaned forward, put my elbows on my knees. Sat there in just my jeans.

"I ask because I've... I've never felt this way, and we've barely even seen each other. Talked. I just assumed this was what it was like for you with the others."

Yeah, I'd had other women, but I wasn't going to go there. I didn't even want to think about any of them because the only face I saw in my mind was hers. "I didn't want a relationship," I admitted.

"I... I didn't realize I was forcing you into one." I heard the prim shift in her voice. I'd pushed a button of hers, and I'd lost some of the ground I'd made. She'd shared more than I'd imagined, and she was backtracking.

"Whoa, princess." I put my hand out. "I said I didn't want a relationship."

"I heard you the first time," she snapped. "You don't have to repeat it."

"Yeah, I do." I sighed, cupped the back of my neck. "I do now."

"Do now, what?"

I realized I wasn't making much sense. "I want a relationship. Now. With you."

Another pause. "Oh."

"Yeah, oh. This—" I circled my finger in the air even though she couldn't see me from the other side of the Atlantic. "—thing we have, it's... fuck, it's more, Harper. I fell fast. You're hard to fight."

"Why me?" she practically whispered. "We don't run in the same circles. You were right."

"About what? That I'm not good enough for you?"

"What? No."

I slid back on my bed, leaned against the headboard.

"The arm patches. Remember when we were walking to pizza, you described what you thought an Art History professor looked like. The guy, the... Larry over here, he wore a jacket with arm patches yesterday."

I could see it. Maybe even a pipe clenched between his teeth. Fuck him for his fucking quickie.

"I have a doctorate in medieval art, for god's sake. I'm afraid of elevators, and I run to escape, but I don't get anywhere. Why, why on earth would you want to be with me?"

I heard the confusion in her voice. She honestly believed—

I wanted to beat the shit out of every single person who made her doubt herself. That elbow patch prick would be the first for only validating that she was only worth enough of his time or attention to get off in some dark corner.

"First off, *you're* too good for me. I have a GED I got in juvie. Barely. I'm not telling you about the shit I've done. Princess, I have a record. Jesus, baby, I fight for a living even though these days they're in a ring, yeah? As for elevators, we can always take the stairs. And running? As long as you run to me, everything's going to be just fine."

She was quiet then, and I felt like shit.

"Princess, don't cry."

I heard her deep breath. "I'm not crying. I told you, I don't cry."

Except with me. She *was* crying, but I wasn't going to argue. She was the strongest woman I knew, and I wasn't going to think less of her if she shed a few tears. But she didn't seem to know that yet.

"When are you coming home? I'm sick of talking to you on the phone, and maybe you're right, we skip the phone sex. You come home, and I'll get you beneath me. The real thing's gonna be better anyway. It will be with me," I added, just so she knew I was different, that *we* were different. "I'll pick you up at the airport."

"I left my car there."

"When?"

"Soon."

"Princess," I said with a warning tone. She was dodging.

"Soon," she repeated then hung up.

Fuck.

16

ℋARPER

MY TIRES WERE FLAT. I couldn't miss it as I walked up to my car in the parking garage.

It was Christmas. While everyone else on the flight was upbeat and cheerful, headed to visit family, I knew I was returning to an empty apartment. No big holiday dinner. No mistletoe or stockings, no Norman Rockwell get-together. No, I came out of customs and didn't find grandparents with glittered posters waiting for me. Instead, I found a special gift, my destroyed tires. Not just flat, but slashed. If that wasn't a sign that Cam was out of jail, I didn't know what was.

I should've spent the flight thinking about the conversation with Reed. I had no doubt he'd be really good at phone sex. Even better at the real thing. What he'd wanted me to do... it still made me hot.

But instead of thinking about his big hands on me, I'd

thought about Cam, and rightly so. I'd had eight hours to watch movies and stew. He was out of prison, and I had no doubt he'd be visiting me soon enough. I just hadn't expected him to slash my tires. I sighed, debating what to do about it.

"We've been waiting for you."

I spun on my heel, my fingers slipping from the handle of my wheeled suitcase, and it fell to the ground in the airport long-term parking garage. The sound of metal on concrete echoed in the huge structure.

My heart leapt into my throat at the sight of the two men. I'd never seen them before, but I knew who they were. Who they worked for. They wore thick puffy coats and black caps, their breath coming out in puffs of white. They couldn't be much older than me, much older than the two who'd tried to assault me in the elevator.

It was much colder here than in London, but I was sweating.

I glanced around, saw other people on the far side of the garage. A car went down the ramp behind me. It was early afternoon, so the space was well lit, well used, but still, they could harm me if they wanted. I took a step back. Then another. They were well out of reach, but with a line of cars at my back, they could easily grab me.

"You had to come home on Christmas, didn't you? My mother's going to kill me for being late for lunch." The guy on the left glanced at his friend, who nodded his head in agreement.

"What do you want?"

"We don't want anything." The guy on the left added, narrowed his eyes. "We're here to give you some advice."

I couldn't breathe. Couldn't think. Just stare into their eyes. Eyes that seemed to have no soul.

"There are cameras," I blurted out, pointing toward the stairwell I'd come out of.

"We're just having a conversation," the same guy said, his hands out in front of him as if he wanted me to come in for a hug. Since I knew that wasn't the case, it was to show anyone who wanted to play back the security films that he wasn't armed, that he'd done nothing more than chat with me.

"I can scream. People will come."

Both just smiled. "Here's the advice, sweetheart. Then we'll let you get on with your life. Give Cam what he wants. Otherwise, the elevator? You won't get away next time." With that, they started to walk away, then the talker turned back. "Oh, your new place? The building looks nice."

I remained where I was, watched them as they walked down the long line of cars and into the stairwell. My heart hammered, and my adrenaline made me shudder. Fuck.

Cam. This all came down to Cam. He was out of jail, and they still wanted something from him. They wanted money. And Cam's money had gone to me. *I* had what they wanted. If I didn't give them the money, Cam would probably be dead. So would I. And so would those in my building. They knew where I lived. They'd been there. Bile rose in my throat at the idea of them watching for me, seeing the others. God, they wouldn't hesitate to hurt Reed or Gray or Emory.

A car drove by, startled me into motion. I picked up my suitcase, speed walked for the stairwell—the one on the far side of the garage opposite of where the men had gone—and went back out to the passenger pick-up area. I didn't give a shit about my car. It was possible I'd have to sell it after this, not sure if I'd ever think the vehicle reliable or safe ever again.

There were lots of people around, airport security just down toward the end of the terminal. I could scream and people would come running. But I couldn't. No one would believe anything I said, and besides, it wasn't like the police could do more than take a report. Slashed tires weren't getting anyone arrested, and neither guy had done anything illegal. Scaring me wasn't illegal. It wasn't as if I could identify either of them. Even if there was security footage, it wouldn't matter.

Slashed tires weren't going to put Cam back in jail or keep those guys from getting to me somewhere else. They knew about my apartment, but from what they'd said, hadn't gotten in. If the one guy's mother had any sway, her son wouldn't be out scaring women for the rest of the day; he'd be too busy drinking eggnog and eating turkey. I had to think I'd be safe in my apartment, or maybe I should just get the next flight back to Heathrow.

My heart rate hadn't calmed. I looked around, frantic and eager travelers swirling around. Families with small children, businessmen heading home. Home. I barely had a home. I hadn't unpacked, perhaps subconsciously waiting for something like this to happen, to remind myself I wasn't staying, that I'd never be able to settle.

With fumbling fingers, I ordered a car, waited.

I was numb. I didn't feel the cold wind. I felt nothing. I was good at that. I'd had plenty of time to perfect taking my emotions and sticking them in a locked box, tossing away the key.

I looked around. I was surrounded by people, but I was so fucking alone. I had no one. My parents chose Cam. I had my friends, but I couldn't pull them into this. And I wouldn't call them on Christmas. I had Reed. Did I? My heart beat faster at the thought of him but realized I couldn't have him. No way.

Not with these men after me. If they knew I was into Reed, if they saw us together, they'd hurt him. Use him to get to me. And these were just the damn thugs. God, if Cam found out about Reed? He was desperate. What was *he* going to do now that he was free? If *he* knew about Reed, I felt nauseated at the thought. Cam would be ruthless and cruel, just like always.

The guys who'd assaulted me in the elevator had waited two years for payment from Cam, and he'd go to any lengths to stay alive. He'd given me to them once, and I knew he'd do it again.

I'd have to let Reed go. It wouldn't be hard. We'd never really been together anyway. Just an emotional moment on my part. Sitting on his lap for an orgasm was what teenagers did. It was quick. Meaningless. And the phone calls, the texts? The sexting? A crush. Nothing more.

I wanted to believe all that, but it was all bullshit. Bullshit so my heart wouldn't hurt as much as I realized I'd somehow fallen for him. I thought of Reed's face, the intense blue eyes, the rarely given smile. The rough hands, yet gentle touch. I swallowed back the ball of tears lodged in my throat.

I'd take the job in London. They'd offered again while I was there. It would be easy. I was all packed. My suitcase, even my apartment. I just had to deal with HR at the university. I could be settled before the next term started. I'd be safe. No one could get to me with an ocean in the way. Even Reed. I just had to stay away from him until I moved again.

Easy.

I just had no idea how I was going to do that.

17

EED

I woke up at the usual time before dawn, even though I'd turned my alarm off just so I could sleep in. For once. Merry Christmas to me. Instead of rolling out of bed, I rolled over.

Four hours later, the apartment was bright, even though the sky was heavy with gray clouds. Reaching an arm out, I grabbed my phone from beside the bed, looked for a text from Harper.

Nothing. Sighing, I ran my hand down my face, wiped the sleep away—and the frustration.

I was whipped. Fuck, this girl had me wrapped around her little finger. And I wanted to be whipped. I wanted *her*. Where the fuck was she and why wasn't she answering my damn texts? She hadn't responded at all yesterday. And today was Christmas, dammit. It wasn't like her. Not lately. I'd gotten her to open up. Hell, I'd gotten her to sext.

She'd refused to do phone sex, which was fine, although

my balls didn't agree. I'd come up with the stupid idea of texting instead. She'd gone for it. I hadn't heard her little pants before she came, the way she would call out my name, but it had been better than nothing. She knew I was a bossy fuck in bed, or in a text, and had liked it.

For long distance sexting, it had been tame. Hell, she'd still had her fucking panties on. I just told her to make herself come. That was it. I hadn't talked dirty to her, told her what I'd do to her once I got my hands on her. None of it.

Harper wasn't a virgin, but she acted innocent with me. As if someone may have had her body before, but she was giving me more. All of her.

She knew how I felt about us... this, knew it was special. I'd even used that word. Yet she wasn't calling me. The plane flight wasn't that long. The last time we'd talked, she'd said *soon*. We needed to have a chat about the definition of fucking soon.

I climbed from bed and went into the bathroom, brushed my teeth thinking about what she'd told me. How she'd lost her virginity at thirteen. I spit in the sink, rinsed it down. Fucking rape.

I found some workout clothes in the laundry basket, tugged them on. Dropped to my bed to tie up the laces on my running shoes. It didn't matter that it was Christmas. I had a fight in two weeks, and I needed to run. Especially if I was eating Emory's mashed potatoes later. And pumpkin pie.

I shoved my hat on, tucked my earbuds in, got my music blasting and set off. Five miles later, my legs were tired, and I was sweating, even though it was below freezing. I stripped off my hat and my jacket, went to the kitchen for a drink of water to take some time to cool down before I showered. It made no sense to do it right away because I'd still be sweating when I was done and have to take another.

As I grabbed a glass from the cabinet, I heard water running. Not loud as if coming from my bathroom, but through the walls. On occasion, I heard it, the pipes coming from Gray's apartment ran behind the center wall. While the building was solid, if I paid attention, it was noticeable. Like now. I had to think Gray had stayed tucked in bed with Emory, savoring a quiet holiday morning with his girl. It made me think of Harper. If she were here and in my bed, I sure as hell wouldn't get out of it for anything. Especially not a five-mile run.

———

I took the stairs down from Gray's and Emory's apartment. While it was only one flight, I felt the fifteen steps or so might help work off the three pieces of pumpkin pie and the pound of mashed potatoes. I hadn't eaten that much in a while and besides feeling stuffed, I was sleepy. I had the plaid flannel Emory had gotten me tossed over my shoulder. It was from her and Gray, but I'd spent most of my waking time with Gray recently and knew he hadn't gotten anywhere near the mall to pick it out.

Standing in the concrete stairwell only made me think of Harper. Where she was, what she was doing. Maybe she'd gone to her parents, spent Christmas Eve with them and stayed. Her car wasn't in the lot—I'd checked like a fucking stalker. I pulled my phone from my pocket, scrolled to her name. Dialed. I went out into the second-floor hallway, grabbed my key from the long chain about my neck to open my door. I heard a faint ring, but it wasn't coming from my apartment. I didn't have a landline. It was coming from

Harper's. I glanced at her door, walked toward it. I looked at my phone, saw it was still connected, but she didn't answer. I ended the call.

The ringing stopped. I pressed her name again. I heard the ringing again. I knocked on the door. Waited.

"Harper," I said, knocking again.

Nothing.

I called her a third time. The ringing came again.

I banged louder. "Harper. Open the door."

I started to freak, coming up with all kinds of shit scenarios. She'd fallen in the shower and hit her head. She'd gotten the flu and was too sick to get to the door. There was no way I was going to let this go. I had to know she was all right.

"Harper!" I made a fist and banged it against the door. "I hear your phone ringing. Let me in or I'm going up to Gray's to get the key."

I heard the bolt turn first, then she opened the door.

My heart settled back into place. "Jesus, you scared me." I said that without really looking at her, but when I met her gaze, I stepped into her apartment, forcing her to step back.

I frowned. She kept her grip on the door, held it open, used it as a shield between us.

"What's wrong?" I asked. I wanted to grab her, pull her into my arms, but the last time I'd done that, she'd sobbed in my lap. Of course, I'd also made her come, so I was torn. I wanted to do that again, but instead of being mad like she had been last time, she looked... cut open. Her hair, usually sleek and long, was up in a sloppy bun. She had no makeup on, and dark smudges marred her gorgeous eyes. While it was December and everyone was pale in Colorado, she looked sickly.

She cleared her throat. "Nothing."

"Are you sick?" I asked, reaching my hand out to touch her forehead, but she stepped back, pulling the door with her. I saw more of the hallway than I did of her. I could see a sliver of an old sweatshirt and pink plaid flannel pajama pants. Thick socks were on her feet. It was the least sexy outfit I could imagine on a woman. Every bit of her curves was hidden beneath the heavy layers, but she looked hot to me. It just made me want to unwrap her to see what was beneath.

She shook her head, loose strands of her hair swirling about.

"When did you get back?"

"This morning." Her voice was flat.

"I thought maybe you were with your parents or something."

"No."

I frowned.

"Why didn't you let me know you were home? I was just up with Gray and Emory. You could have joined us."

"I was tired from the trip."

"Why don't you come over to my apartment? I don't have much, but I can make you some toast and tea. I won't burn that."

She didn't even smile at my shit cooking skills.

"We can take a nap together." The idea of climbing into my bed and wrapping her in my arms sounded like heaven. If we were naked while doing it, so much the better.

"No. It's best if you go."

I took a step toward her, but she held up a hand, and I stopped. The last thing I wanted to do was spook her.

"Please." I couldn't miss the frantic tone of her voice, the wildness of her eyes.

I glanced into her apartment. It looked as if she hadn't

touched any of her boxes or furniture since the movers dropped it off when she moved in. There were no pictures on the wall, no lamps lit to fight off the growing darkness outside. She had been away, but I didn't even see a TV.

"You're just going to spend Christmas alone?" I'd enjoyed the afternoon with Gray and Emory, her son Chris. Even her old neighbor, Simon, came to watch football and eat. They were more family than any blood relatives I ever had. But seeing Harper like this, something bothering her and alone, pissed me off. Not at her, but she shouldn't be by herself. No one should be alone on Christmas.

"Yes."

I shook my head. "Princess, I can't let you do that. Come over, yeah? Besides, I've got a present for you."

It wasn't much, something silly really, but I couldn't not get her something.

She shook her head even harder now. "No. I'm going to sleep. It's seven hours ahead, and I've been up forever."

"That's not it." It wasn't.

She pinched her lips together into a thin line.

"After all the phone calls, the texts, you're going to shut me out?"

I watched her throat as she swallowed, blinked hard. Looked over my shoulder. Anywhere but at me. "You should go. I'm... I'm taking a job in London. It would be best if we ended... it now."

I felt as if I'd been kicked in the gut with a wicked side kick.

"It?"

"Our—" She cleared her throat. "—friendship."

"That's what you think this is?" I tried to keep my voice steady, but it was damn hard. I didn't want to scare her, but I was practically vibrating with frustration. "A simple friendship?"

I could see it in her eyes, knew she was right there with me, but something was up.

"Did someone hurt you?"

She looked away. Not like before when her eyes glanced around, but she turned her head to the side, blocking me out.

"Harper. What the fuck happened?" Yeah, I hadn't meant to swear, but if I touched her, she might freak. I had to let my frustration out somehow, like a slow bleed. Someone had hurt her, but she wouldn't say. "Tell me."

"No. You need to go."

My gaze raked over her, but the only skin I could see was her face and neck, her hands. "Did someone touch you? Professor Arm Patch?"

"No!" she said, her voice finally full of life. It was anger, but it was something.

I took a deep breath, let it out. "Someone hurt you in England, and you're going to take a job over there?"

The idea of her going back overseas made me want to rip the fucking door off and pull her into my arms to let her feel how it could be when we were in the same room. When she was pressed against me, she could hear my heart beating out of control.

"It's not like that."

"Then tell me."

I watched as her grip tightened on the doorknob as if it were the only thing keeping her from coming to me. "No. You need to go. Thank you for... being there for me. I won't bother you anymore."

"Bother me? You think you're *bothering* me?" I groaned, ran a hand through my hair, then stepped toward her.

She pointed to the hallway. "Go."

Her control was slipping. I could see it. Somehow, I knew every little nuance of her, even when she was putting up a fucking brick wall. With razor wire across the top.

"Fine. I'm going, but this isn't over."

I stepped into the hallway, trying to think of something to say to get her to open up, to tell me what the hell was going on. She finally lifted her eyes to mine. There, I saw hurt. Desperation. Need. Longing.

It was in her eyes and in my heart. I'd opened up to her, to someone, and she was pulling this shit. Fuck no. She was the first person who I'd connected with, who I cared about, and she was shutting me out? I wanted this to work. Needed it to because I needed her. Hell, having her reject me now felt worse than any beating I'd taken, whether in the ring or in a dank alley.

"Harper—"

I lifted my hand to reach out to her, but I yanked it back when she slammed the door in my face.

18

*H*ARPER

I CRIED. I'd thought I'd been alone before, but when I shut Reed out of my apartment, it felt as if I'd put more than just a door between us. He'd told me on the phone there was more to this... this thing between us. He hadn't even wanted a relationship at first, and then he'd changed his mind. Reed, the guy who had ring girls tossing their panties at him, wanted me. Me! Somehow, even being across the Atlantic, he'd changed his mind. Wanted something real.

The first guy ever who wanted me for more than a quick fuck, and I pushed him away. All because of Cam. I couldn't risk Reed getting hurt because of me. I couldn't live with myself if something happened to him. I *could* live with knowing he was safe. Barely. I'd leaned against the door, ensuring I didn't rip it open and run to Reed, tell him I was sorry and jump into his arms. I slid to the floor, sat there and just cried. Cried like I had when I'd escaped from the elevator two years ago.

I'd told Reed I didn't cry, that there weren't any tears left. I'd been wrong. So wrong.

My cell rang again. I looked up, knew it was sitting on a small table by the door. Traitor. Reed had heard it, knew I was home. My heart leaped at the idea of it being Reed, so I scrambled to grab it.

It wasn't him. Some local number I didn't recognize. I pressed Ignore, then scrolled through the missed calls. Nine of them. Two had been from Reed just a little while ago, but before that. More.

Cam. And he hadn't called on Christmas to wish me a happy holiday.

It had to be him. If the guys from the airport said I should give Cam what he wanted, then he'd be calling me to get it. Especially now that he was out of jail.

The ringing stopped. But he wouldn't. Cam wouldn't stop until he got what he wanted from me. Money. It was all about the damn money. I could just give it to him, make him go away. But he wouldn't. He never would. He'd used me his whole life.

I thought about what I'd told Reed, about my first time. I hadn't thought much of it, not until I'd spoken the words aloud. I remembered. Cam had given me to his friend. For sex. I just had to wonder if Cam owed him too, and I'd been payment. Even at thirteen.

I rubbed my arms, a coldness settling over me. Cam had pimped me out, just like he had two years ago. Reed had seen it right away, but I hadn't. Maybe I'd blocked it out, made it less than what it was to save my sanity. But that was gone now. *Everything* was gone now.

Somehow, I crawled to my bed, tossed the covers over

my head. Wallowed. Cried some more. Darkness settled over the apartment, but I was afraid to turn on the light, worried that the guys from the airport were outside, looking up and maybe wanting to get to me. At some point, I fell asleep. I didn't dream, didn't even stir, perhaps thanks to jet lag. While I'd slept hard, I woke up before five, wide awake. The time change was messing with me, and I knew it would for several days. It was still dark, and I was still afraid to turn on my lights.

Between semesters, there wasn't any work to do. No papers to grade, no meetings to attend. I couldn't even go into HR and resign. All the offices were closed until after New Year's. I thought of Reed, just a wall away. Wondered what he thought of me. How was I going to face him? To know he wanted something more, and I'd have to lie, to have him hate me to keep him away from me. If those goons saw me with him... I shuddered at what they might do.

I had to do something, or I'd go stir crazy. I'd lose my mind. Worse, I'd cry some more. Grabbing some workout clothes from the pile on the floor, I got dressed, put on my running shoes. Without looking toward Reed's apartment door, I ran down the emergency stairs and to the gym. The front desk opener looked up when I came in. He was just turning on the computer, having just opened at five. Since early morning wasn't my usual workout time, I'd never seen him before. I introduced myself, grabbed a towel, and went over to the row of treadmills. I put my earbuds in, set the program and began, lost myself in the rhythm of the music, the pace of my feet slapping against the moving belt.

Gray stepped into my line of sight, carefully as not to scare me. He was dressed to work out. Outside. Running pants, a fleece pullover, a black skull cap instead of his Stetson. None of it hid his fighter physique or the hours he spent working out along with his clients. With Reed. His pale eyes met mine, and he waited patiently for me to tug out my earbuds, push the buttons to slow down to a walk.

"We're going for a run outside. Join us."

I glanced over my shoulder. The gym had a few people working out on the machines. I could see a yoga class in the private room, everyone sitting cross legged, their back twisted to the right. But I didn't care about any of that when my eyes latched onto Reed. I almost stumbled at the sight of him, dressed for the weather as well and leaning against the front desk.

"I'm good here," I said. I was warmed up, my skin damp with sweat.

He shook his head. "We need you to set the pace. Push us. Three miles." He offered me a slight smile. "You can do that without breathing hard."

He glanced down at the display on my treadmill. I followed his gaze, saw I'd already gone almost three already.

The way he looked at me, I felt as if I couldn't say no. As if I were one of his clients. I wasn't. Far from it. I ran from a fight. As I told Reed, I ran from everything. I hadn't talked with Gray much, only met him with Emory last month to see the apartment and to sign the lease. And then pizza with them and Reed.

"Please. Reed's company is boring."

He may have been trying to get a smile from me, but it didn't work. I pushed the End button, and the machine stopped. I gripped the bar to steady myself.

I stepped down, ran my hand over my sweaty face and followed Gray over to where Reed stood, his ice blue gaze focused squarely on me. He was so handsome, and I couldn't believe he wanted me. He was well aware how fucked up I was, and yet he wasn't running away. No, he was a fighter. I saw it in the rugged hands, the broad shoulders, the powerful jaw. Yet, I knew what was beneath that. I felt as if he'd shared more with me over the phone than he had with perhaps anyone else. Maybe even Gray.

I wanted to run to him, hope he opened his arms for me, and let him hold me. To hope he never let me go. God, he was so hard to fight. I wanted him, needed him, even after only being with him for a short time. We'd talked, texted and sexted while I was gone, but together in the same room? Less than two hours, perhaps. Still, I knew I wanted more too.

But it wasn't to be. I felt pretty confident that five-thirty was too early for either those guys from the airport or for Cam to mess with me, but that didn't mean when they had their coffee they wouldn't. We stopped in front of Reed, and he looked me over with a quiet intensity that made me want to squirm, Gray remaining silent beside him. Reed just gripped the hem of his long-sleeved fleece, pulled it over his head and handed it to me.

It was the second time he'd seen to my comfort when going outside, and I took it, worked it on. It was still warm from his body, and it smelled like him. I resisted the urge to grab the collar and pull it up and over my nose, to breathe him in. Just like last time, he silently rolled up the sleeves. His gaze shifted from his task to meet mine. I'd all but forgotten Gray was there when he walked toward the doors that led to the parking lot.

Reed slipped off his hat, placed it on my head himself. Seemingly satisfied, he picked up his earbuds which now dangled from the neck of his t-shirt, settled them in place. He wasn't talking to me. I didn't blame him, but with the music in his ears, he wasn't able, or ready, to hear anything I had to say.

We went outside, Reed holding the door for me. I took a deep breath of the cold air, let it out. It felt good on my heated skin, but I was happy for the hat and fleece. I flicked a glance up at him. He was watching me still, but there could've been a whole ocean between us instead of two feet.

"Okay with our usual three miles?" Gray asked, blowing into his curled-up fingers.

"Sure," I replied. My legs were loose, limber, and I was far from done.

"Give us a few minutes to warm up, then set the pace. We need to work off some pie."

At the mention of Christmas dinner, I glanced at Reed again, but he was scanning the parking lot.

Gray started running. I tucked my earbuds in and joined him. Reed came up on my other side, so I was flanked by both of them as we turned onto the sidewalk. I followed Gray when he turned corners, very aware of Reed beside me, but only picked up the pace when he signaled me to do so. It was only then that I got into my usual groove, turned my mind off and forgot about Reed. Forgot about everything, the steady beat of the music in my ears helping me keep pace. The men kept up as we ran, ending back up at the gym as the sky had a hint of color to it. Instead of going inside, I walked in a circle in the lot, continuing to move. I was winded, but not done. No, the pace, the fresh air, and especially Reed beside me, only had me itching to keep going. The three miles only proved that even off the treadmill, I couldn't outrun my problems.

When Gray said something to me, I plucked my earbuds out. "You're not done, are you?"

His skin was a ruddy red from the cold, from the workout, his dark whiskers a strong contrast. He was breathing hard, but not sucking wind.

"I'll just go back to the treadmill," I said, looking up at the sky.

He held up his hand. "Wait."

I watched as he went into the gym.

Reed stood, hands on hips, a few feet away. Earbuds dangled from his collar. I could hear his ragged breathing, see the sweat on his T-shirt. He'd said he didn't like to run, and it was obvious the pace was faster than he was used to. I couldn't last three minutes in a round with a fighter. No way. He looked quite a bit like when I'd first met him. Sweaty and tired from a workout. Then, he'd scared me, and I'd wanted to get away from him as fast as I could. Now, I wasn't afraid of him. I wanted him with an ache that made me put a hand to my chest.

I wanted to tell him I'd lied, that I wanted to be with him. It wasn't over. I didn't know how it could be over, but he'd never believe me now.

"Run with Carter and Paul." Gray's words had me turning my head. Two guys I'd never met before were coming out the door after Gray, but I didn't work out in the mornings. They were lean and muscular, clearly fit and spent plenty of time at the gym.

"Hi," I said.

One gave a hand lift as a wave, the other nodded.

"They're two of my guys and need your quick pace. Do the same loop. You remember it?"

I nodded, tugged Reed's hat down on my head.

Gray stepped back. "Good. See you in... twenty-two minutes or so."

Carter and Paul looked at Gray as if he were joking about the just-over seven-minute mile, but when he slapped one of them on the back—I wasn't sure which was which—they eyed me with suspicion.

"If you need another three miles, I'll have two more guys run with you."

"It'll be light by then, I'll be fine." They'd done enough already.

Reed crossed his arms over his chest as if settling in for an argument, but Gray responded. "No. I'd like it if you had company. Besides, my guys need the harder workout."

I glanced between all four men. None spoke up, most noticeably Reed. His expression hadn't changed once in the past half hour, but I had a feeling he wanted to herd me back inside. Paul and Carter seemed to be waiting for orders from Gray, tall sentries flanking him. I felt like I had a bodyguard rotation, but there was nothing I could do about it. All four of them were big, solid, and the way I knew they could fight, no one was going to lay a hand on me.

But seeing Reed made me ready to run more, to try to block out everything, including him. I turned and started out of the lot, the new guys hot on my heels. If they needed a push, I'd give them one. Besides, the only way I was going to feel better was if I felt nothing at all.

19

EED

"I CAN'T JOIN TONIGHT. My legs are killing me," I told Seth, who ran the BJJ class. He was in his white gi and black belt, standing just outside the door to the room. It was wall to wall mats since the class was completely on the ground, unless he was teaching takedowns. And then, there was no fucking way I could get up and down for an hour.

"Heard you had a ruthless trainer." He wasn't talking about Gray because he wouldn't have grinned. The ass-kicking Harper had handed to a bunch of us this morning had made its way around the gym. Seth was about five years older than me, was some kind of tech nerd and knew his shit when it came to Brazilian Jiu-Jitsu. He wasn't a fighter and had no interest in MMA, although I knew he participated in BJJ specific competitions.

When I thought of Harper, I didn't think ruthless, but the pace she'd set on our three-mile run was faster than I liked. Hell, I'd hated every minute of it after the first block. But I'd had no intention of leaving her side. The only perk behind the twenty-some minutes of pure lung torture was that I'd gotten to watch her body, see the way her leg muscles flexed and pulsed as they pumped out the distance. Her chin had been up, her arms at her sides, she'd been in the zone, something like I got into once I stepped into the ring. Nothing was going to stop her or slow her down.

By the time we'd turned back into the parking lot in front of the building, I was all but ready to collapse. I wanted to stay with her, to be near her and figure out what the fuck was going on with her, but there was no way I could have made it another three miles at her pace. But she hadn't been done. Winded, yes, but she had the determination and drive as if she were only in round two of a five round match. Gray had seen it and, thankfully, forced Paul and Carter to run with her next.

Yeah, they'd been as finished as me when they'd returned. The sun had been up then, and Gray'd had Tom and Drew ready to do a third lap although they hadn't been as eager seeing the four of us on our return. But they'd have gone because everyone did what Gray said, and it proved all of us had shit for endurance.

"She showed us," I admitted.

"You did, what? Your usual?"

"Three miles."

A student came up, shook Seth's hand and went in to stretch before class started.

"How far did she end up doing?" he asked.

"Twelve miles, maybe." Once she was done, she all but dashed for the stairs to her apartment, and I'd seen nothing of her since. I had no idea where her car was, but I'd been in the gym all day—either training with Gray or working with my own clients—and hadn't seen her come back out.

Seth just smiled and shook his head in a combination of wonder and insanity over her skills. I shifted, my legs aching. I had to wonder if her legs were as rubbery as mine and if she needed those muscles rubbed. My dick twitched. I had to shut that shit down.

She'd made it more than clear the night before that she was done with me, that she didn't want more. She hadn't been thrilled about it; the look on her face said she was tormented. While it should've made me feel better, she felt as shitty about this as I did, it didn't. I wanted her to be happy. Preferably with me. Something was up, and I was going to give her space. Although she said she was moving to the UK. No, she was *running* to the UK. I just had to find out why before she did.

"Hey, Reed." I turned around to see Jack from the front desk coming my way. "You wanted me to let you know if that car was out there again."

I looked over his shoulder and toward the lot. I was too far away to see anything, but the cars parked directly in front of the building. I'd barely slept the night before, I'd all but sprinted three miles beside the woman I wanted but couldn't have and now this. I'd played it straight, played it cool until now. Yeah, I'd left them alone before, but I wanted to rip their heads off. I couldn't handle this shit with Harper and keep my head on straight for the fight, especially if the opponent was trying to dick around. Harper was more of a head game than any shit Dominguez could toss my way.

Gray rapped on the glass of his office window, redirecting my attention.

He was on the phone and gesturing me his way, but I waved him off and stalked right outside. There they were.

Same car, same assholes from the other day. When I approached this time, the driver rolled down his window. I put my forearm on the roof of the car, leaned close.

"What the fuck does Dominguez want?" I asked. I didn't have time for this, for them. Out of the corner of my eye, I saw Gray standing by the hood, a few others from the gym, too.

The guy frowned then smiled. Yeah, the stupid-ass gold tooth. "Who the fuck is Dominguez?"

I reached in, grabbed him by the collar of his coat and pulled him partway through the open window. Without a seat belt on, it was easy to do.

"Hey man, what the fuck?"

Carter moved to stand by the passenger door, keeping the other guy from getting out.

"The fight's in a few weeks. I'd say it's square. Legit even. What do you want from me?"

I tightened my fist, tugged him further, so I was all but breathing on him.

"I don't want anything from you," he spat out. "Shit, why would I fuck with a fighter? I'm here for the girl."

My brain shut down for a second. Girl?

"Who?"

I saw Gray tense, which was practically impossible since he never offered anybody any kind of tell.

"The girl. The professor."

My blood should've run cold at what he'd said, but instead it ran hot. This feeling, the seeing-red rage, it had been a long time since I'd felt this way, since I was a teenager. Since I'd murdered my father. I wanted this asshole dead for even thinking about Harper.

Curling my arm, I pulled him through the window even

more until he was wedged. "Talk. Now. I've killed before, and I *will* fucking do it again."

His eyes bugged out, and his face was turning an off-putting shade of purple. "My boss wants her," he gasped.

"Why?"

"Her brother."

"He should go after her brother then." I had no idea what the fuck he was talking about. All I knew was that there was no way they were getting their hands on her. Taking her to their boss? Fuck, no.

He shook his head, tried to wriggle to get more comfortable, but his arms were pinned at his sides inside the window opening. "She has what they both want. They tried, two years ago."

I let go, stepped back. For a second, the guy hung in the window, but then began to shimmy back into his seat. Turning to Gray, I watched as Thor came around me, reached in and grabbed the keys from the ignition.

"That was Quake Baker on the horn. Had some info for you." He tilted his head toward the guys in the car. "Asshole's telling the truth. They tried for her before."

The guys in the car were forgotten. I glanced up at Harper's apartment on the second floor. I bolted toward the building, practically ripped the door off the hinges as I entered the lobby. I tugged my key pass from around my neck, slapped it against the sensor on the wall then took the steps two at a time. Banging on Harper's door didn't bring results.

"Harper!"

I waited, tried to catch my breath. Remembered what she'd said to me in this spot the day before.

It would be best if we ended it now.

She hadn't said she wanted to end it. She'd said it was for the best. I'd been too angry to process her words.

I banged some more. "Open the door, princess. I know you're in there."

Nothing.

"I know about your brother." I didn't, but I had to hope he was the reason she'd shut me out. The reason she was scared.

I was about to knock again when I heard the lock snick.

The door opened, and I didn't give her a chance to shut me out again. I took a step toward her, picked her up without slowing and carried her across the room.

"Reed!" she cried.

I wasn't putting her down. No fucking way. I breathed her in her scent. Some kind of fruity shampoo and pure Harper. I felt her lean muscles, her lush curves.

I glanced around. "There's no place to sit," I said, frustrated.

"I haven't unpacked."

That was obvious and only prompted me to what she'd said. She was leaving, taking the job in the UK. Why should she unpack?

"Why is it so dark in here?" I asked, going to the light switch on the wall.

"Don't!" she said, her body tense. She grabbed my wrist before I could touch it.

I stilled, looked down at her. Saw the panic in her eyes. Felt the anger coursing through me. "You don't want them to know you're here, do you?"

She shook her head. Bit her lip.

Jaw clenched, I spun about, carried her out of her apartment. The door had never closed behind me.

"I can walk!"

I ignored her, tugging it shut with one hand as I carried her to mine, then set her down long enough to unlock it. Carrying her to my chair, I sat down, settling her on my lap. With one arm about her waist and her head tucked beneath my chin, I just held her.

And breathed.

"Reed."

"Give me a minute," I said, shutting my eyes.

This. This was what I'd been wanting. No, needing. Ever since she'd cried in my lap last week, I wanted her right back here in my arms. She was safe. I didn't want to talk. I just wanted to hold her, kiss her, hell, sink into her sweet pussy. But no. I had to know what was going on before we could move forward. While she'd opened up to me, there was a shit ton of stuff left unsaid.

I sighed, felt her warmth seep into me. "Tell me about the guys in the car."

She stiffened but didn't move. "They're here?" she whispered.

I pushed her away from me only enough so I could tilt my head down, meet her eyes. "Now? Yeah. Several other times." She glanced away, and I gently turned her chin back, so she had to look at me. "Who are they?"

"I... I don't want to talk about it."

I looked between her eyes, saw the fear, the anguish. I wanted to take that away.

"Don't?"

"Can't."

I brushed my thumb over the little indent in her chin. "Why?"

She sighed, lifted her hand to cup my jaw. It was the first time she'd touched me, initiated the contact because she wanted to. She was studying me as I had her. "I don't want you hurt."

She doesn't want me—

Something broke in me then. I'd been trying to stay two steps ahead of my past for years. First the military then training with Gray. I fought and fought to escape what I'd done, what I'd become. In and out of the ring. I'd done all that because I wanted to be better than the boy my parents had done shit to raise. I'd even thought I'd done a damn good job of breaking away from it all.

But now? Harper's words changed it all. *She didn't want to hurt me.* If she knew my past, knew what I was capable of, she'd know that was impossible. I could take care of myself. I had my whole life. But now I wanted to be the man she saw.

Somehow, Harper recognized something in me that I didn't. That no one else did. And that made me want to prove she wasn't wrong, that I really was the guy she saw. There was nothing on earth that would stop me from kissing her. My mouth met hers, and for a second, she was stunned. So was I. It was better than I imagined, that kept me awake at night. Her lips were so soft, just the feel of them against mine had me groaning. I cupped the back of her head, held her there, gently. Reverently.

This.

Fuck, *this.* I kissed across her closed mouth, learning every bow and curve from corner to corner, flicking my tongue out to lick, taste. When she opened for me, I didn't hold back. I took, but I gave, too. Fuck, this was what I'd been aching for since the moment I saw her. All the time, I knew she was thousands of miles away, and I couldn't touch her. I'd wanted to ease that fear, even of a damn elevator, and I'd ease it now. As long as she was sitting in my damned lap, everything was going to be fine.

She whimpered and began to shift in my lap. There was no chance she could miss how hard I was. I wanted her. Literally ached with the need to be inside her, but it wasn't the right fucking time. When I claimed her, I wanted her mind solely on me. Hell, I wanted her mind completely blank.

I pulled back but held her head still, took in how her long, dark lashes were fanned over her pale skin. Her eyes opened slowly, met mine.

"Hey," I murmured.

She offered me a small smile—this time genuine. I loved the way her cheeks flushed, and her eyes had lost the fear.

"This... thing between us?" I slid my thumb over her cheek. "It's my job to protect you. That's how this works. You give me your problems, and I take care of them."

She licked her lips, and I stifled a groan. "Just like that?"

"Just like that. Do I look like I'm not strong enough to take care of you?" Her gaze raked over me, and she shook her head, her silky hair sliding over my fingers. "Tell me."

She looked down, but I wouldn't have it. I easily lifted her, so she straddled me, but this time she was wearing a pair of black yoga pants and a thick hoodie sweatshirt. My hands went to her hips, held her in place, but my thumbs stroked over her taut muscles. She wasn't going to avoid me any longer.

"Beautiful, tell me."

"I told you about my brother, at least a little bit on the phone."

I wouldn't forget what he'd done, giving her to his friend to fuck.

"He's always been in trouble of some kind. Cheating in

school when he was a kid. A gambling ring in high school. He went to three different prep schools before he graduated because he kept getting kicked out. He went out of state for college, so I don't know much of what he did there, but I'm sure it was a lot of the same thing. Only worse."

I watched as her throat worked when she swallowed.

"Two years ago, he got in over his head with this guy. Owed him tons of money." Her dark eyes met mine... then dropped,,, then she lifted her chin, so she looked at me dead-on. "I was at a family wedding. A distant cousin. One of the hotels in downtown Denver. I was leaving, going to my car in the parking garage. Cam was there with some men, but I ignored them. I... I don't like my brother, so I always stayed away from him."

I didn't say anything, and I tried as hard as I fucking could not to grip her hips. I had an idea of what was coming next, and while I didn't want to hear it, to know it had happened to her, it had to come out. Like a damn splinter under the skin.

"The men—not Cam—got in the elevator with me. They stopped it between floors and... came on to me. Said they were taking me back to their boss as payment, but they'd try me out first." Her eyes went hazy at that, as if going back to that moment in her mind. "I... I panicked, obviously. The one who'd been touching me, I kneed in the crotch. He let go, fell to the floor. The other guy grabbed me, and I fought him. He ripped my dress. It's a blur after that, but I jammed my stiletto into the top of his foot. It stopped him long enough, so I could push the button to get the elevator moving. I swiped all the floors, and the door opened. By then, one of them had me, and I fell. I screamed, kicked and got away. The doors closed, and I was on the valet level of the parking garage, and they'd continued down. People were there, and I got help."

Fuck. No wonder she was scared of elevators and freaked out the first time she saw me.

She took a deep breath, all of that having come out in a rush. "The men got away."

"And your brother?" I stroked my thumb over her cheek.

"When I told the police what happened, that my brother was behind it, my parents got involved. Got him out of the charges by saying I'd willingly gone off with the men."

My thumb stilled, and I couldn't help the way my fingers gripped her hip. "Your parents said that? They chose your brother over you?"

She nodded. Her hair was sloppy, as if she'd fallen asleep with it wet at some point, but I wanted to touch it, so I tucked a tendril behind her ear. "They always have."

"You flew home on Christmas because..."

She bit her lip. "Because I was spending it alone. At least on the flight, they gave out free drinks."

"Beautiful," I said, drawing out the word on a sigh. I pulled her head in, our foreheads touching. I could feel her heat, her breath. "All you had to do was come to me. I was waiting for you."

She pulled back her eyes wide with fear again. "That's just it. I shouldn't be here. They'll hurt you."

I couldn't help my eyebrows going up. "The guys in the parking lot?"

"They said they'd been here, but I just hoped maybe they were wrong. If I kept my lights out, stayed hidden, they'd give up."

I frowned. "You kept your lights out?"

She nodded. "I didn't want them to know I was home— they might try to get in."

This was so fucked up. Especially since she thought she was alone in this. Dealing with these assholes.

My mind churned through everything she said. "Wait. What do you mean they said they'd been here? You talked to them?"

Now she looked away. "They were waiting for me at the airport. They... they slashed my tires."

I knew the men were long gone from the lot by now, Gray and the others ensuring it, but I wanted to hunt them down and kill them for fucking with Harper. It seemed I had to make a list of who to hurt. Her brother, her parents. Those assholes who slashed her tires.

"Why now? If they got away with it two years ago, why are they back?"

"Cam. He's out of jail."

"I thought your parents got him out of his involvement with your assault." I bit out the last few words.

"He was, but a week later, after he was cleared, he was arrested for drug possession with intent to sell. My parents... well, my dad, who's a lawyer... got it lowered to a misdemeanor. Cam had no choice but to do two years."

"And?"

"And he's out now. But those men? They never got the money Cam owed before he went to prison."

I couldn't help but frown. When I thought she had some issues, I had no idea it was like this. And she wanted to push me away. "Okay, but why go after you? Why weren't they waiting for your brother when he walked out the prison gates?"

"Because they know he doesn't have the money. He probably told them I had it to keep himself alive."

To keep himself alive and put the heat on his sister. The fucking asshole.

"Do you have the money?" I was so confused. Why the hell was she mixed up in this? This mess was between a loan shark and Cameron Lane.

"Yes."

I lifted her up enough, so I could slide out from beneath her, turned her so she was sitting in my chair, and I paced.

"You have money Cam needs to pay off his debt? His two-year-old debt?"

She nodded, curled her feet beneath her.

I ran my hand over the back of my neck. "When did you talk to him last?"

She looked as if she were scrolling back through a calendar in her mind. "Actually, it was right before I met you. The elevator panic attack. He'd called me, and I'd been upset, decided to run it off."

Yeah, I could see now why she liked to burn off the angst and why she could run marathons.

"Like I said, me having the money is why he's still alive, at least I assume. If they'd killed him in jail, they'd never get the money. I guess they're patient, or they expect a lot of interest, but now that he's out, they want it."

"And Cam?"

"I haven't talked to him since that time, but he's left messages, texted. Telling me to give it to him."

"I assume you haven't." If she had, they'd leave her alone. No airport visits. No slashed tires. No parking lot surveillance.

She dropped her head back against my chair, closed her eyes. "That money? It's hush money from my parents. My *payment* for my elevator experience. Cam knows they gave it to me and told me, at least the last time I talked to him on the phone, that I owed him. It was all because of him that I had it, and I should share some of it with him."

I stopped directly in front of her, leaned down and put my hands on the arms of the chair, so we were eye to eye. "Your parents gave you money to drop the charges against your brother for giving you to a fucking loan shark and his... his goons as payment?"

I knew my voice was loud, that I could hide my anger no longer, but she wasn't scared of me. No, she cupped my damn jaw again. "Now I have the money to save Cam from those men."

My eyes widened, thinking the worst. "You're not going to give it to him, are you?"

"And enable Cam like my parents? No. That money's tainted." She shook her head. "I won't touch it. I'd rather move to the UK than do anything with it."

"You'll hide in your apartment with no lights on until it's time to move?" She blushed at that. "I thought you said you were tired of running."

Her chin came up. "I am, but every time I try to get on with my life, things keep messing it up. Do you think I wanted to be given to those men? Do you think I want my parents to call me and tell me to come to a party celebrating Cam's release from prison? Do you think I want to have a brother like him?"

She moved to stand, and I let her go. She began pacing. I watched her get mad.

Finally. This was what I wanted. Harper mad. Pissed. So angry she stood up to her brother, to her parents, to those fuckers who assaulted her, instead of running.

"Do you think I want my tires slashed? That Cam calls and messes with me? I don't want that. I don't want any of it."

On one of her passes, I grabbed her arm, stopped her. "What do you want?"

Her eyes dropped to my mouth. "You, but I can't have you."

Hope replaced all the anger. My heart leaped, not from panic or worry but from something else. Something new. Something... pure. She wanted me. I couldn't help but grin.

I put my hands to my chest. "I'm right here. I'm all yours."

Her gaze dropped to my mouth, then I saw disappointment fill her eyes as she turned away from me. "Do you know what those men will do?"

"That's why you pushed me away yesterday. You're afraid those guys will hurt me."

She nodded. "If they discover we're... together, then they'll hurt you as pressure for the money. I don't want them seeing anyone but me."

I closed my eyes, opened them slowly. I took her hand, lifted it to my cheek again, held it in place. Her skin was so warm, and I seemed to hope her goodness would seep into me.

"I'm a professional fighter. Look at me. Do you think so little of me that I can't protect myself and you? What about yourself?" I wondered. "Aren't you afraid?"

She gave me a sad smile. "Afraid? I've been afraid for two years. The only time I haven't been afraid is when I'm with you."

20

$\mathcal{H}$ARPER

I TOOK in the dark scruff on his jaw, the curved muscles of his defined shoulders beneath his T-shirt, the broad chest, narrow waist. He wore dark gym shorts and running shoes. He wasn't sweaty like after a workout; his clean scent was heady. So was the intense promise in his eyes. I put my hands on his arms, felt the bulging muscles of his biceps, slid them down over the corded forearms to link my fingers with his.

I was riled, tense, angry. Reed had made me talk, forced me to tell him the truth. All of it. And yet, he was still here. He was strong. Strong enough for both of us. And yet, he lifted our linked hand to his lips and brushed a kiss over my knuckles. I felt it, like a jolt of sizzling electricity throughout my body. Strong yet gentle. He was unlike anyone I'd ever known.

"I just want you, too," he murmured.

"But you don't just get me. You know my problems, Reed. This is why I've been pushing you away."

"Why we haven't had phone sex?" he asked, the corner of his mouth tipping up.

I couldn't help the smile his teasing words brought about. "I... I want you, but—"

With our hands tangled, he quieted me with a kiss. When he lifted his head, he brushed my nose with his. "There are no buts right now. Just us. You're with me. You're safe."

I sighed and nodded, my nose sliding along his cheek, the whiskers there ticklish yet soft. The one urgent kiss now wasn't enough. He was right in front of me, touching me, our breaths mingling, but I needed more. Turning my head slightly, our mouths met. I was tentative for a split second, a wisp of a thought that Reed might not want more flitted through my brain but was erased entirely when he dropped my hands and pulled me into him, one arm sliding down to grip my ass, the other cupping the back of my head.

He took over, dominated the kiss. And me. It felt so good to be held, as if I were so thirsty for contact. I was, actually. *Real* contact. For once, I didn't hold back, and I opened for him, letting his tongue dip inside my mouth, find mine. He learned me, one delicious lick at a time. I whimpered, my skin heated, I relaxed, every tight line in my body curved and blurred.

I hadn't realized we'd even moved until Reed broke away and dropped into his chair but kept an arm about my waist, so his face was in line with my hoodie-covered breasts. He kept his eyes on mine as he worked my sweatshirt up my body. I lifted my arms to help him then saw out of the corner of my eye when he dropped it to the floor.

"You're wearing too many clothes," he said, his voice a frustrated growl as he took in my T-shirt and yoga pants.

"So are you."

His eyes flared with heat. With another one of those small smiles, he reached behind his neck, tugged off his shirt, dropped it on top of my hoodie.

"Like what you see?" he asked. It was only then I realized I was ogling. His body was tight with muscle. Shoulders round, neck angled. There was a smattering of dark hair on his chest that tapered down to his navel. The eight-pack of abs was impossible to miss. But it was the tattoos, the one that wrapped around his upper arm and down over his shoulder to just above the flat, dark disk of his right nipple that had me reaching out. My fingers hovered, worried I shouldn't touch.

But when he grabbed my hand, pressed my palm against his hot skin, he groaned, and I gasped. When I didn't move my hand, he did it for me, roaming over every perfect, chiseled inch of his torso. Only when I caught on to what he wanted did his eyes fall closed and his hand dropped to his lap.

Oh yes. Complete access to touch and study Reed's body? It was my turn to groan. At least drool. His lips were slick and red, his nostrils flared as he breathed, his hands gripped his knees as if trying not to grab me.

"Harper," he said, my name almost ripped from his throat. When he opened his blue eyes, he looked at me with a need so intense it stole my breath.

Two fingers gripped the hem of my T-shirt, and I felt the rough brush of his fingertips on the bare skin of my belly. I gripped his hand, stilled his fingers although when I thought about it, he wasn't moving them. My eyes met his, and all of a sudden, I felt vulnerable.

But he deserved the truth. "I've... I've never let a man see me before."

He frowned, a deep crease forming in his brow. "But you've—"

"I've had sex, yes, but it's always been quick, with clothes on." I tucked my lower lip between my teeth. "Or, only took off what was required. So...yeah."

I sighed as Reed dropped his hand.

"That's not how it is between us, is it?" he probed.

I shook my head, tucked the hair that had come out of my bun behind my ear.

"I won't take what you're not willing to give," he said. "But I want all of you. I want to see you, touch you. Have you in my bed. I don't want anything between us, not even clothes."

His voice was even, steady. I could step back if I wanted, to stop what we were doing. But after the past week, distance was gone. Secrets were gone. Everything was gone that separated us except for our clothes. He already saw me. Even the darkest spots within.

"You don't have to hide yourself from me, but when you're ready. If that's not—"

I ripped my T-shirt over my head, let it fall to the floor, but that spurt of bravery disappeared, so I covered myself with my arms.

I met Reed's gaze. He didn't look away, didn't look lower. "Beautiful," he said.

I loved that he called me that, but I didn't think he meant it now. "You aren't even looking."

He slowly shook his head, gently gripped my wrists from beneath my neck and uncrossed my arms, lowered them to my sides. "I don't need to."

I was before him in my bra and my black leggings. I should be shivering, but I was far from cold.

Finally... finally his gaze dropped, and I watched his face, watched his jaw clench, his pale eyes darken to a stormy sea blue. "Is this what you wear underneath those professor clothes?"

He raised his hand and with just the tip of his finger, traced along the edge of my pale pink bra. It was fine, sheer mesh, so nothing was hidden. I didn't have to look down to know my nipples were hard.

"Except when I run, but yeah. I... I like lingerie."

I had a drawer full of it. No one had seen any of it but me. Until now.

He grunted as his finger slid from the swell of one breast, into the valley between and over the other. I wasn't overly large, a full B cup, but Reed seemed to be just fine with that.

His touch slid down my belly to the edge of my leggings. "Do your panties match?" He flicked his gaze up to mine, and I had a feeling he might cry if I said the wrong answer. I nodded, and he gave me a wicked grin. "Show me?"

I couldn't resist that smile. They were rarely given, and it felt good to know I could make him happy. He wanted me, wanted to see me in just my skimpy bra and panties and more, but he was still letting me decide. To set the pace.

I climbed from his lap, stood before him. With my hands at my hips, I shimmied out of my leggings and pushed my socks off at the same time. When I stood back up, he looked his fill, his penetrating gaze roaming over every inch of me. I felt exposed, vulnerable, but at the same time, cherished.

Leaning forward in the seat, his arms came around me like steel bands, pulling me into him, so his cheek rested between my breasts, his hands at the small of my back, but his fingers angled down over the curve of my butt. My hands flew to his shoulders. The feel of his hot skin against mine had me gasping. His lips brushed the inside curve of one breast before he pulled back enough to begin kissing me. The under curve of my breasts, across my belly, my navel and around. He didn't once touch my nipples, and I was growing impatient. Antsy. Needy. His mouth was hot, fierce and gentle at the same time. Little licks spread heat and then coolness as he dampened my skin. I had no idea when I threaded my fingers into his hair and began to press him closer, but the whimper of his name had him lifting his head.

"Yes?" he asked. His eyes held such promise, such intense need I could only give one answer.

"Yes."

With his arms still banded about me, he stood and lifted me up, carrying me into his bedroom. He seemed to like carrying me around. It made the differences between us so obvious. I wasn't short, but I felt small and feminine in his strong arms. He laid me on the bed, lowering himself to hover over me, keeping his weight off me with his hand beside my head.

The light wasn't on, so the room was bathed in a soft yellow glow from the other room. I could see Reed clearly, but part of his face was in shadow. It had only been a week, and only a few hours of that in each other's company, and yet I wanted him. I wanted *this*.

"I've never done it like this before," I admitted.

His eyes roamed over my face.

"Missionary?"

"When it means something."

He sucked in a breath then lowered his body, so we

touched from chest to hips. Shifting my legs, I made room for him to settle between my thighs as he kissed me.

With the soft bed at my back and a very solid Reed on top of me, I was just where I wanted to be. I felt safe. So very safe. And he was right. There was nothing between us.

21

EED

FUCK.

She was so soft, so sweet, so perfect beneath me. Reaching up, I carefully worked the tie from her hair, so it was loose across my pillow. My fingers were blunt and clumsy, afraid to snag all that silky softness. I breathed in the scent of strawberries. I met her eyes, held them.

Yeah, this fucking meant something.

"No more running, princess."

Her pink tongue darted out, licked her lip. "No more running," she whispered.

"I'm here, yeah?"

She gave a slight nod. "Don't... don't leave."

I stroked her hair, this time catching it in my grip and tugging lightly, so she couldn't look away. "I'm not going anywhere."

She frowned, and I pushed on.

"I want everything from you. *Everything.* The difference between me and your family is that I'm not going to take. I want you to give it to me. Yeah?"

I was a selfish fuck. I wanted every bit of her. Her body, her mind, her heart. *Her soul.*

"You're not like them," she whispered. "You're not anything like them. You're giving yourself in return."

I couldn't resist, leaning down and kissing her forehead. "That's right. You've got me. The good and the bad. The stuff you don't know about."

Her hand came up, cupped my jaw. "I know you're good."

I was the one to look away. "I'm not, princess."

"Tell me then."

She was beneath me in my bed, my hard dick pressing into her, and I was going to have to bare myself to her. I could shed my clothes, I didn't give a shit about modesty, but baring my soul, to have her know how bad I really was, it was heavy.

I wouldn't take her until she knew the truth though. I wouldn't be like her brother, like that asshole who took her virginity. She needed to be with me, completely, knowing everything.

She'd shared her secrets with me, and fuck, I had to share mine with her. That way if she had to walk away, she could because once I sank into her, she'd be mine, and there would be no going back.

I shifted, so I laid beside her, my head propped up with my hand. I swirled a finger around her navel.

"I grew up, like you, in Denver. A different part of town. A *very* different neighborhood. My mother was an alcoholic who slept with a bottle of whisky. Forgot about me. Food. Clothes. My dad worked a long line of dead-end jobs, got fired from every one of them. Took it out on us. When that didn't bring in the cash he wanted, he broke the law. He took me with him on armed robberies."

Yeah, that was when she sucked in a breath, her belly stilling beneath my fingers. She didn't say anything, so I pushed on.

"By the time I was twelve, I was his getaway driver. I could just reach the pedals, and I was an accessory to state and federal crimes."

Her mouth fell open.

I lifted my gaze from those lips, met her dark eyes. "I killed him. My father. When I was seventeen. We'd come back from a botched job. He got drunk, hit my mother. By then, I was too big for him to fight—I'd learned some things on how to defend myself on the streets, the playgrounds. But when I protected her, he came at me with a tire iron. She ran out. I'd heard later she went to the corner bar to forget it all in the bottom of a bottle of Jack. Left me to fight him on my own. He broke my arm before I got the weapon from him, turned it on him, knocked him out. The cigarette he'd been smoking fell, and it set the cheap carpet on fire. I walked out."

She just stared at me, wide eyed. Yeah, now she knew the real me. All of it.

"I killed my father and got a stint in juvie for it, Harper. And I'm what you want?"

Her eyes were wide as she processed my words. Now, I knew her childhood had also been shit. Money sure as fuck didn't buy happiness, but she'd had clothes, food, the finest schools. She hadn't had love. Neither had I.

"Reed," she whispered.

"You stayed good. You didn't sink to the same shit as your brother, as your parents. I did."

She shook her head, then pushed at me, so I'd move. She sat up and straddled my waist, forcing me to roll from my side onto my back. I set my hands on her thighs, looked up at how fucking gorgeous she was.

Every inch of her was blemish free, inside and out. She was like an angel in her pretty bra and panties, as if just putting my hands on her would get her dirty.

"You're not what you say. Not even close."

My fingers gripped her hips.

"You said I was smart—I know things. I know you're good—you helped me. You could have taken from me, fucked me that night you found me with Larry. Could have let me blow you like I'd tried."

My dick hardened at those crude words coming from her lips.

Her hair slid over her shoulders as she shook her head. "You didn't. You're honorable. Brave."

"I'm not good enough for you," I said, getting the rest of the truth out.

Her dark brow winged up. Slowly, she shook her head, her hair sliding over her shoulders, some of it falling down in front, the ends of it touching the swell of her breasts.

"You don't get to decide that for me. You don't get to tell me how I feel about you."

"Gray saved me."

"No. No way. You saved yourself."

My thumbs slid over her silky skin. "I met him in the army. In fucking Afghanistan. We grew up within two hundred miles of each other, and we met a world away. Told me to look him up when I got out. I did. He gave me an outlet for all my shit. Now I only fight in the ring. With rules."

She licked her lips as she just stared down at me. I waited for her to climb off my lap and leave.

"What happened to you wasn't your fault. You were a kid."

"So were you, princess," I said, my voice soft.

Her eyes flared at what I was talking about, and she nodded. Swallowed hard. "You went to juvie because of your dad's actions not your own."

"I killed him," I said, gripping her hips hard.

"Would you still call me princess if you knew I wanted Cam dead?"

Besides my dad, her brother was the only other person I ever wanted to see dead. What he'd done to Harper as a girl... fuck, and even now.

"You don't want his blood on your hands." I jackknifed up, so she was still straddling me, but we were nose to nose. "You're too good for that."

I wasn't. I'd see her brother pay. Killing him would be a fucking pleasure. I'd only let out my anger, my violence in the ring now. I'd make an exception though.

Fuck, I never imagined there would be someone who meant enough to go back. Harper was the only one who I'd ever do it for. I'd kill for her. No question.

"So are you," she said, lifting a hand to stroke over my head, down my cheek.

I didn't say anything because we could argue about this all fucking day, and what a waste that would be. I'd take care of Cam, but there was no fucking way he'd get between us now.

Not here in my bed. Banding an arm about her waist, I rolled us, so she was beneath me once more. Eye to eye.

She'd never bared herself to anyone before. She'd do it with me now. I doubted she'd ever fucked in a bed. If she had, it had been quick. This wasn't going to be fast. I had her where I wanted her, and I wasn't letting her up for anything.

I met her dark stare. Held it. I saw into her so far. Past every wall she'd ever put up.

"There you are," I whispered, staring down at her with wonder. "All for me."

I lowered my head, kissed her. Kissed the fucking hell out her. She may have said the words, but I wanted to prove how different I was than the guys from her past. I wanted to wipe them from her mind with how good it was going to be.

I wanted to show her what it was supposed to be like. So I would, too.

My mouth slid along her jaw to the spot behind her ear. I licked down her neck, feeling how she shivered, how she caught her breath. When her fingers clenched on my arms. I wanted to know what got her hot.

Her skin was like silk against my lips, the upper curves of her breasts above her bra sweet heaven. With a flick of my fingers, I opened the front clasp.

"Beautiful."

"Reed," she breathed then gasped when I took a nipple into my mouth. It hardened against my tongue, her fingers rubbing over my scalp. My hair was too short for her grab, but she held my head there.

I looked up at her face, saw the way her eyes were closed, her mouth open, chin tilted toward the ceiling.

I kissed across the valley between her breasts to her other nipple. Played with them, back and forth, until she writhed beneath me. Her legs parted, and I settled between. I was in no rush to go past this. Fuck, I could play with her tits all fucking day. But it was all about Harper. My dick could wait, or I'd come in my fucking pants if I had to. She came first. Always.

I slid lower down her body, swirling my tongue around her navel, then along the edge of her panties. As I did the last time, I touched her through the sheer fabric. Gently, lightly, and I looked up her body to watch her reaction.

I had no idea if something would set her off, if I'd trigger a memory that might freak her out. "You good, princess?" I asked, looking up her body from the most perfect place in the fucking world.

She pushed up on her elbows, looked down at me. Flushed cheeks, hard nipples, taut belly. Fuck me.

Her eyes narrowed. "What are you doing down there?"

"You good?" I asked again.

"I'll be gooder if you would get with it."

I grinned then. "You've got a fancy doctorate and all you can come up with is gooder?"

"Yes," she snapped.

"I'll stop anytime you want, just say the word. Any word."

"Okay," she said, softening a little.

I held her gaze as I hooked my fingers in delicate edge of her panties and slid them down. She moved her legs to help me get them off, then with a flick of her foot, tossed them off the bed.

"I'm not going to break, Reed," she said.

I watched her for a second longer, then even more.

"Reed," she repeated, almost begged.

Her saying my name was like a bell at the beginning of a round, starting a fight. I focused on the task at hand, gave it my all. Won.

I slid off the bed and to my knees, grasped her ankles and pulled her to the edge. Pushing her thighs apart, I looked my fill, took in how pink she was. How wet. How perfect.

Then I put my mouth on her and got her taste all over my tongue. Worked her until she was clawing at my shoulders, crying out my name, her knees all but squeezing my ears.

She was going to come on my tongue and fingers before I got in her. I'd get her soft and ready for me because I was big, and I was primed.

I'd wanted her since the moment those elevator doors opened. But no guy before had gotten her off, seen to her. Made her scream. They'd satisfied a need in her for a connection but nothing else. It hadn't been real.

This was. Her responses to me. The way her pussy clenched around my finger as she came. As she dripped all over my chin.

Fuck yes. She was incredible. Responsive. Passionate. And she made me feel like the champion of the world because I'd given it to her. Her first man-made orgasm.

She'd give me all the rest, too. Every single fucking one belonged to me.

22

*H*ARPER

GOD. Reed. He was... this was... I couldn't think. I could only feel. Feel his body pressing into mine. Feel his heat, his strength. Feel his intensity, his desire for me.

How had this guy gotten past every defense I ever raised? How did he see things no one else did?

Why did he even want me? He knew every broken piece of me, and he was still here. Sure, it could be for the sex, but he'd touched me and never asked for reciprocation. Even now—

I moaned, low and deep, coming hard. Coming all over him.

He didn't let up, licking and kissing my core as the best orgasm of my life slowly faded. I was relaxed—biggest understatement ever—and boneless. Sweaty. Content.

He came up over me, wiped his mouth with the back of his hand. "Good?"

I rolled my eyes, and I couldn't help the smile. "Looking for praise?"

He didn't say anything, only winked.

"I've... I've never had a guy do that before."

He frowned down at me. "No one's ever—"

I shook my head.

"Fuck, princess. I'd live between your thighs if I could. I love the taste of you on my tongue."

I could feel the blush that spread, but he was right, there was nothing between us any longer. "Do I get the taste of you on my tongue?"

He groaned, and his hips thrust into me. I could feel how hard he was through his gym shorts.

"Not this time, princess. I want to come buried in that gorgeous pussy this first time."

I didn't think gorgeous was the adjective I'd use, but if he *finally* wanted to get inside me, I was all for it.

I slipped my fingers into the waistband of his shorts and pushed them down, suddenly frantic for him.

"Easy, I'll get in you. Yeah?"

He pushed back and climbed from the bed. Stripped. When he was bare, he gripped his dick and stroked, eyeing me. Just as I was him.

This was the first time I'd seen him like this. God, he was perfect. Muscled and toned, there wasn't an ounce of fat on him. He didn't think he was smart, but just looking at him, I knew he took his profession seriously. His body was his job. I'd never seen him in the ring, but he knew what he wanted and went after it. Took it seriously and gave it one hundred percent.

Just like he was with me.

He was all in, just as he'd said.

Going around the bed, he opened the bedside drawer

and pulled out an unopened box of condoms. "Got these for you," he said as he opened the box, pulled out a strip. "I never have anyone here. Just you."

He ripped one off, left the rest on the bedside table.

I watched as he rolled it down his length then grabbed me, moved me up the bed, then came over me once more.

I couldn't help but touch him, to run my hands over his bare chest, slide over his lean hips, cup his taut ass.

"Fuck, you're killing me."

Lowering to his forearm, his eyes met mine once again. Held. "Ready?"

I bit my lip, nodded. He was ensuring I was right there with him.

Reaching down between us, he notched the head of his dick at my entrance. Without looking away... without even blinking, he watched me as he slowly filled me.

A whimper escaped, and I clenched down around him. He felt so good, so big.

"Fuck, you're perfect," he said again. He held himself still inside me, and I didn't like that. He was being too nice.

"More," I said. "Please."

He pulled back, thrust deep. Watched.

I lifted my hips, met him. "More," I said again.

He did it once more.

I grabbed his butt and pulled him toward me. "Harder."

He wasn't going to let go unless I told him to, worried I'd cry or fall apart. That wasn't going to happen now. No way was he giving me sweet.

"Fuck me, Reed."

His eyes flared with heat, and he gave me one more study then tangled his fingers in my hair, tugged slightly, then let go.

He gave up the fight then, his need taking over.

Thank God.

He took me hard. Fast. Deep. He leaned down, sucked on a nipple. Nipped at it. Sweat dotted his forehead. His breathing was ragged as if he'd fought in the ring.

But it felt so fucking good. I rocked my hips into him, met him with every hard thrust. Called out his name, clawed his back.

Came all over him, and with a roar, he came with me.

He fell on top of me, kept his weight off with his forearm, caught his breath against my neck.

He was in me, around me. Everywhere. I felt like we were one. I'd never been so close to someone before. Never wanted to. I didn't want Reed to move, to leave. To even blink.

"That was round one, princess," he said into my skin, idly stroking my sweaty hair back. "As soon as I can see again, get ready for more."

———

REED

I WOKE up at my usual time like clockwork. The sky was still dark, but today, for the first time ever, I had someone in my bed. I had Harper.

I didn't want to get up and leave her. She was bare, tucked into me, and my arm was slung over her waist, cupping her lush tit. My dick prodded her ass, ready for more. But I'd taken her twice during the night, and I felt fucking proud of myself that she was now down for the count.

I wasn't letting her go back to her apartment. Hell, she'd

be lucky if I ever let her out of my bed. Now that she was here, everything was different.

I wasn't going through the motions anymore. I had a purpose. Making Harper happy.

Fighting wasn't a way to get my aggressions out any longer. Sure, I made cash through my fights. I'd been saving it, living in this apartment, working as a trainer while I was Gray's fighter.

I wouldn't be one forever, and the money would see me right for the future. Until now, I'd had no idea what that looked like. But now all I saw was Harper's face. Her smile. The way her eyes widened with wonder when she came on my dick.

She'd set me free. But she wasn't free. Not until her brother was handled. Until he was gone for good. I'd see it done, even if it took me back out of the ring to fight. To turn back to what I'd been raised to be.

I'd gone to jail once for killing someone. I wouldn't hesitate to do it again. Harper was the only person who I'd break my rules for. Who I'd chance everything I'd made. Who'd make me be everything I'd fought so hard to leave behind.

Slowly, I climbed from the bed, careful to not wake her. She sighed and rolled onto her stomach. The smooth line of her spine had me pulling up the covers, ensuring she didn't get cold with me gone.

I padded to the bathroom, took a piss and brushed my teeth. After I threw on some clothes, I went downstairs. Found Gray in the gym waiting for me, leaning against the counter reading what looked like a piece of mail. He glanced at my bare feet, then at my face.

"I'm out today."

"Harper?"

"Yeah. I'm going after a guy. Just wanted you to know."

He didn't react, only arched a brow. "She's in trouble."

"Yeah."

"The guys out in the lot?" He tipped his head in that general direction.

"Her brother. Makes those guys look like Boy Scouts."

He dropped the paper onto the front desk, then cut around it and into his office. Flicked on the lights, then settled into his chair. The place was quiet, the early morning crowd slowly staggering in.

"Shut the door."

I did then leaned against it.

"Tell me."

I did, leaving nothing out. I gave him what I knew, what I planned on doing. All of it.

He didn't say a word until I was done.

"You're willing to throw your career away, everything you've done, for her?" He leaned forward in his chair, eyed me. We'd known each other for years. Hell, he'd *saved* me. It was a dick move for me to trash all that he'd done for me. But it wasn't for me. It was for Harper.

"Fuck yeah."

He nodded, pushed his chair back and stood. "Okay. But this shit is bigger than you can handle on your own."

"Gray—" I began, but he cut me off with his hand going up.

"No one fucks with our women. I get that."

Yeah, he definitely did.

"But you going after Harper's brother solo is suicide. If Mommy and Daddy got him out of what he did, they'll find a way to toss your ass in jail. Not going to happen. You worked too hard to give that shit up. You're not going back to that shit and for a good reason. But that asshole's going down. We just need some help."

"We?"

He narrowed his eyes. "We. What? You thought I'd toss you out on your ass? Tell you you're blowing your career for pussy?"

I pushed off the door at that, narrowed my eyes.

"Not going to happen. You get a girl, you hold on as fucking tight as you can. She got shit going on? You deal with it for her. Yeah?"

I sighed, nodded. "Yeah."

I couldn't help the smile. Gray didn't back down from a fight, not even one like this far outside the ring. I shouldn't have even thought that shit about him.

"I know just the guy," he said then glanced at the clock. "Normal people aren't up at this hour. Give me a few."

I left him, for once skipping my training for climbing back in bed. I had a reason, and he knew it. Just for today. That's all he'd give me. That's all I needed for her to know I wasn't going anywhere.

Took the steps two at a time back to my apartment, stripped and slid back in bed, pulling Harper close. She stirred then rolled over, still in the circle of my arms. Dawn cast her in a soft light, and I could see the smile on her lips, her sleepy eyes. Her hair was a mess and fuck did she look beautiful.

"Morning," I whispered.

She kissed my chest then pushed off me and climbed from the bed.

"Where you going?" I wasn't letting her leave if that was her intention.

"Bathroom. Got an extra toothbrush?"

I cracked a smile, relieved. "Under the sink," I called as

she shut the door behind her. I tucked my hands behind my head, stared up at the ceiling.

When she came back out, I held up my hand. "Wait."

She stopped halfway back to the bed. "What?"

"Gotta look my fill." I took in every inch of her. Those perfect upturned breasts, narrow waist. Long, muscular legs. She was gorgeous, and she had no fucking idea.

And she was mine. All mine. No one had ever seen her like this before. Bare. Exposed. Real.

She rolled her eyes, did a little spin and then came over to me, her cheeks a pretty pink. I pulled back the sheet and blankets, and she climbed back in but straddled my waist. My hands automatically went to her hips. Settled.

"Where'd you go?"

My fingers slid along her hips, her ass. "Talked to Gray."

"You don't need to train this morning?" She cocked her head, and her hair slid over her shoulder, the strands brushing her pink nipple.

I stared at it as I replied. "I've got a different kind of workout planned."

"Oh?"

I rolled us, so I was above her, my leg nestled between hers. "Yeah. It's going to be sweaty. Breathless."

"Hard, too?" she asked, shifting her hips.

I angled mine into her, nudged my dick against her thigh. "Very hard."

"Mmm," she replied, her hands sliding down my back as eager as me. Fuck, now that I showed her what it was like, she was insatiable. Fine by fucking me.

I nuzzled her jaw then worked my way down her body, licking and kissing my way down to her pussy. Her fingers moved to my head.

"Where... are you going?"

Settling between her thighs, I looked up at her. Yeah, I could live here all fucking day. "Gotta warm up first."

She huffed out a laugh, but it turned into a moan when I licked into her. She didn't say anything at all after that except for my name when she came all over my mouth and fingers. Only then did I know she was ready, that she was soaked and soft for me. Then I took her. Made her forget everything but me. Made her know who she belonged to. Who was fucking her. Keeping her. Giving her everything.

23

HARPER

A FEW HOURS LATER, we were in the Double B Diner, waiting to meet the president of a motorcycle gang. I was tucked in beside Reed, his arm slung over the back of the booth, his fingers grazing my shoulder. No one sat across from us, and with his size, I could barely see anyone else in the diner around him.

"You said this place is owned by a motorcycle gang?" I asked, looking around. There was nothing about the restaurant that made me think that. It was a typical vintage diner that had been built decades ago, probably when the highway was built. Central entry, booths lining the walls all the way around. Counter seating around the center. We were tucked in the back corner. The table's surface was orange laminate, and there was a small jukebox on the wall next to the sugar packets and salt and pepper shakers.

It was busy, full of a mix of locals and those stopping for

a break on their drive. While Brant Valley wasn't huge, I'd never been to the place before since it was on the far side of town from the university.

The scent of grilled onions and bacon made my stomach rumble. I'd worked up an appetite with Reed. While I ran every day, muscles I didn't even know I had were sore. I couldn't help but smile. Perhaps that was what a slew of orgasms made me do.

"Club," Reed replied. "They're a club although from the limited info I have on them, they skirt the line on the law."

"This guy, he's friends with Gray?"

Reed had told Gray about my problems. At first, I'd been annoyed, but I quickly realized he deserved to know. Guys had camped out in his parking lot. Guys who wanted to hurt me if I didn't give them money. I wouldn't blame him if he hated me or kicked me out of the apartment for bringing trouble to his doorstep. Instead, he'd offered his help.

Help in the form of a guy who ran a motorcycle gang. *Club.*

The waitress brought over the coffee we ordered in a big carafe and two mugs. She set a bowl of creamers beside it then left.

"You heard what happened with Emory last summer?"

I nodded, reaching for the carafe and pouring the dark brew into our mugs.

"Quake Baker helped. He's the president. She's sort of under his protection, which covers Gray too although he doesn't need it."

"Why?" I asked, stirring my coffee. "I mean, how do they know each other? Quake and Emory?"

"She helped his grandson. The kid and his uncle live a few blocks from her old place, and I guess he got scraped up riding his bike. He's... eight maybe. He takes care of those who take care of his family."

Emory was a helper and a mother. I had no doubt she'd taken care of the boy if he'd gotten hurt. She'd even mothered me a bit, getting me into the apartment in Gray's building.

"What does this have to do with me?" I blew on the coffee, took a tentative sip. Even though I'd also lived near this guy's son and grandson, I hadn't known them. Hadn't helped them in any way.

He looked down at me. "Your brother—"

Reed was interrupted by a guy who slid into the booth across from us. I pegged him in his fifties with graying hair and a weathered face. He was tall. Fit although a bulky guy. He wasn't lean like Reed, but I had no doubt he could hold his own in a fight. He wore a black waffle knit t-shirt and jeans.

He set his hands on the table and nodded at Reed.

Reed made introductions. "Quake, this is Harper Lane."

Quake eyed me, as if sizing me up. "Heard you got a family issue."

I couldn't help but laugh at that then shut it down. "Sorry. Yeah, right, a family issue."

He leaned in, his dark eyes pinned on mine. "Reed told me all about it."

My mouth fell open, and I glanced up at Reed. "You did?"

"When you were in the shower. Figured you didn't want to give him the recap."

Yeah, that wasn't something I wanted to do, to share my messed-up life with a stranger, even one who was probably even more rough around the edges than me.

"I don't stand for that shit," Quake said. "Sorry about the language, but you got dealt a bad hand."

I nodded. "Yes." What else was I to say?

"I've got connections. Got a hit off that plate number. The guy who your brother owes? Name's Kevin Randolph. A big-time bookie. Deals with all kinds of gambling. Cards, sports, you name it. The guys who came to your place are his." He cocked a brow, leaned forward, so his shoulders were up by his ears. So we wouldn't be overheard although there wasn't anyone at the table behind us. "He goes by Randy. I know him."

Setting my mug down with a thunk, the hot liquid sloshed over the top. Oh shit. I pushed against Reed to get out of the booth. "Let me up."

He set his arms on my shoulders, gave a gentle squeeze. "Whoa, what's the matter?"

I tipped my head toward Quake. "He knows the guy. This... Randy guy who sent men to *collect* me for him. Tried to rape me. Slashed my tires. Showed up at my apartment. He *knows* him."

"Hold up, doll," Quake said, raising a hand. "I know a lot of people. We're not BFFs or anything. Far from it. I'm not here to hand you off to him. I'm here to help."

Reed kissed my head. "Shh. He's going to help," he repeated. "You think I'd put you in danger, princess?"

I took a deep breath, let it out. With shaky hands, I lifted my mug, took a sip of coffee. No, Reed would never put me in harm's way. "Sorry," I whispered, trying to calm my racing heart.

"Your problems, princess, are mine to take care of." He'd said that before, but this time it was different.

I swiveled in my seat to face Reed head on. "Wait, that's not what that means. I don't want you going after them!"

He looked at me evenly. "I can take care of myself. And you."

"This isn't the ring. This isn't the same kind of fight."

"I'm better in a fight out of the ring. No rules."

I blinked. He was serious. Ruthlessly so. "You walked away from that."

"I did, but this guy and Cam? They need to be taken down."

He was willing to fight dirty for me. To risk everything he'd built for me. I glanced down, then back at him. "Yeah, but they're... they're... bad, and you're not."

Reed winked. "Yeah, princess. I am bad. Just not with you."

"And so am I," Quake added, ending this line of talk. "I'll set up the meeting, make it happen. We'll get you in front of Randy, tell him you're out and redirect his focus where it belongs. On your brother."

He made it sound so simple.

Reed stilled, leaned in. "Hold the fuck up." He tipped his head toward me. "She's not getting anywhere near the asshole. His men tried to *rape* her."

Quake's eyes flicked between the two of us, and his jaw clenched. "Yeah, that's something I'll take care of."

"You're gonna need to get in line, yeah? I'm taking care of it first. You can deal with what's left."

"What? No," I said, but the guys were staring at each other, doing some kind of man-mind melding thing and hadn't heard me.

"I'm all for a meeting with Randy," Reed's tone was laced with fury when he said the guy's name. "But she's not getting near any of them." He thumbed in my direction.

"She's gotta go," Quake countered. "We have to make a deal. Giving him the brother instead of her."

I wasn't sure who was going to win this fight, and I tuned the two of them out as I drank my coffee and thought about it all.

Randy wanted my money. Money that Cam owed him. I wasn't going to give it to Randy. His intimidation tactics so far hadn't worked. Oh, they'd worked, but not for me to hand over the cash.

"Randy uses intimidation to get what he wants," I said out loud.

Both guys quieted.

"What?" Reed asked, looking my way. He stroked my shoulder to tell me he was paying attention.

I glanced at Quake. "I would assume that intimidation works when there's something at stake. That's how guys like this work. Why Cam—my brother—is freaking out."

He gave a single nod. "Yeah."

"People will hand over cash to Randy because they don't want a family member or friend or loved one to get hurt."

"That's right," Quake responded, but I could tell he was waiting to see where I was going with this.

"I have no reason to give this Randy guy the money to save my brother. I don't love Cam. I don't even *like* him. He got himself into this mess and should face the consequences."

"So he sent his guys to try and intimidate you," Reed said, catching on.

"But that's not working either," I said. They scared the shit out of me, but I hadn't given in.

"Not with me around," he vowed.

"Exactly. You've got me protected, and he has no leverage with me when it comes to Cam."

"Go on," Quake said, eyeing me with curiosity.

"He wants the money. He obviously thinks I have it since

he keeps coming around. I doubt Randy's threatening my parents. What if I really don't have the money?"

"You mean spend it?" Reed asked.

I glanced up at him. "I'll give it to you."

He pushed me back a little, so he could turn me to face him. My knee came up onto the booth's cushioned seat. "Whoa, princess. I don't want your money."

He sounded insulted. "Yeah, but—"

"Why haven't you touched any of it?" he asked, cutting me off.

"I told you. My parents gave it to me as payment for what Cam did. Hush money or whatever you want to call it. It's tainted."

"So I should have it? I might only have a recliner and a bed, but I'm not broke. I'm not taking anything from those fuckers. I won't take anything that hurt you."

God, that was... sweet. My heart didn't have a chance around him. Over and over, he proved himself more honorable than anyone I knew. He'd been the only person to ever stand up for me. Protect me. Be with me or do something for me without any reason or motive.

"Then... then I'll give it away," I replied, thinking of an alternative. "A charity. For kids."

Reed's eyes widened then changed. Got darker. Smoldered. Something. He leaned in and kissed me. Not a gentle in-a-restaurant peck but a kiss with tongue. Right in front of Quake, who started laughing.

Reed pulled back, didn't pay him any attention. "I like that, princess. Give it to a place that helps kids, so they have a better chance than we did, yeah?"

I nodded, blinked back tears then smiled. "Yeah. my parents will hate it, which means it's a great idea."

Reed huffed out a laugh then kissed my forehead.

"I'll set up a meeting," Quake said. "Reed, she has to go. If you donate the cash, there's nothing you have for them." His eyes narrowed. "Except your brother. You could give *him* to Randy."

That, I'd be fine with. More than fine. "How can I give him Cam?"

"We'll ensure Randy knows you don't have the money. He might not believe you, but he'll believe me when I say you're out."

Reed nodded. This was what Quake was for in all this. I didn't know anything about him or the MC, but if Randy was afraid of Quake, then he had to be more dangerous than I imagined. His reputation as a badass went even further than I thought.

"That you're under my protection. No one fu... messes with anyone under my protection." Quake took a deep breath, and his chest expanded, showing how fit he was. How strong. How much of a badass I expected him to be. I was glad he was on my side. I had no idea why he was willing to protect me specifically, but I wasn't going to ask.

"Cam won't know we're meeting with Randy. He won't know shit," Reed added.

"Exactly." A waitress stopped by with a fresh carafe, and Quake offered her a smile. "Thanks, doll."

"We set Randy straight then give Cam to Randy. You wanted me to stay out of it, to keep my hands clean, then this is the way to do it. Let Randy do the dirty work for us. Then we're out," Reed said, tipping my chin up, so he looked me in the eye. "Yeah?"

Reed wasn't going to have to fight Randy and his henchmen. He wasn't going to have to fight Cam. I didn't have to worry about him going to jail for doing something to protect me. I nodded. "Yeah."

Then I'd be free. I wouldn't have to run any longer.

"Now what?" I asked.

"I set up a meeting with Randy," Quake said. "Give me a day or two."

"What should I do in the meantime?" I asked Reed. He hadn't let go of my chin. Hadn't stopped staring at me.

The corner of his mouth quirked up. "I can think of a few ideas."

 EED

THE BJJ CLASS WRAPPED UP, and I headed out to the front desk and grabbed a towel from the pile. I watched Harper from across the room as she ran on the treadmill. She looked exactly as I'd left her an hour earlier although she had a pink flush of exertion, and her t-shirt clung to her sweaty skin. I had no idea how she didn't go insane with boredom running for that long. There was nothing to see outside since it was dark out, and the bright lights of the gym made the window in front of her like a mirror.

It'd been two days since our meeting with Quake. I hadn't let Harper out of my sight. We'd had a service fix her flat tires, and we'd driven her car back to the building. It sat in the lot, but I didn't give a shit if Randy's annoying minions or even Cam Lane found it. They weren't getting in the building or near Harper. Gray knew what was up and had spread the word to staff and a few of the guys. Harper was well protected. Not that I was letting her out of my sight.

It was pretty easy to accomplish since we spent most of the time in my bed. Even now, as I leaned against the counter and just... stared at Harper, I wanted her again. Fuck, was she amazing. Incredible athlete. So fucking smart. Brave. Stronger than she ever imagined. And gorgeous.

She had no idea how perfect she was. The way a few of the guys eyed her as she ran reminded me I wasn't the only one who was interested. But I was the one in her bed. I was the one who... hopefully, was in her heart.

I knew her. She'd let me in. Gave herself to me when she'd never offered to anyone before. I wasn't talking about her body but her soul. I'd gone from an asshole who hadn't given a shit about anyone to a pussy whipped guy who thought of love and the melding of souls. If one of the guys could hear my thoughts, they'd wonder if I'd been hit a little too hard in the head.

I'd watched Gray fall for Emory. He'd gone down hard and fast, and no one dared call The Outlaw pussy whipped. He was. Boy, he sure the fuck was, and he'd proudly admit it.

The fucker Larry made his approach from the free weights to Harper. I pushed off the counter to step in but stopped. Watched. Harper'd taken care of herself just fine before me. I couldn't take care of all her problems no matter how much I wanted to. I also wanted to see what she'd do. It had been a week or so since she'd dragged Larry to the stairwell, but so much had changed since then.

I might be confident in the ring, but with Harper, I was just a guy whose woman was too good for him. While I might be spouting poetry and making Valentine's cards with glitter, Harper hadn't said she felt the same way. She'd said she was right there with me but still. When she looked

Larry's way still running at an all-out pace, she pulled out an ear bud to hear what he had to say. She shook her head, and he walked away.

I couldn't help but smirk, and when he walked past me to head to the locker room, I offered him an all-out grin.

Fuck yes.

She'd shut that shit down because she was mine.

I grabbed a towel for Harper and took my time to make my way over to her, watching the play of her toned muscles as I went. Her ass... fuck, it was a work of art.

I leaned against the window in front of her. She was breathing hard, sweat dripped down her temple. A smile tugged at her lips as she took her ear bud out again.

"Hey there. What's your name?" I asked her.

She quirked a brow but kept on running. "Harper," she replied, her voice catching as she breathed hard.

"Really? I thought it might be Angel since I think you fell from heaven."

The stupid joke had her stumbling, and she slapped her hand on the treadmill's control to slow it down. When she was walking at a cool-down pace, she said, "Are you trying to pick me up?"

I winked. "If you have to ask, I'm not doing it right."

Her gaze raked over me in appreciation. "I'm sure you *do it* right. In fact, I am warmed up and ready to go," she replied.

It was my turn to falter because I hadn't expected that awesome comeback. My dick was instantly hard and gym shorts did nothing to hide it. I had to hold my towel in front of it. She saw the action and smirked.

I looked around. No one was nearby, but I stepped closer, resting my forearm on the treadmill. "You need it, princess?"

She bit her lip and nodded.

I didn't look away from her, just reached out and grabbed the emergency release cord and tugged. The treadmill immediately stopped.

I handed her the fresh towel, and she stepped off and wiped her face as I cleaned down the machine for her. When I was done, I led her out of the gym, through the hallway and used my keycard to get into the stairwell.

As soon as the door slammed shut behind us, I tugged her around and into my arms. Kissed her. We were both hot and sweaty, but I didn't give a shit. I wanted her, and I wanted her here and now. I wasn't pressing her up against the cinder block wall. I wasn't fucking her into the stairwell. So I broke the kiss, sat down on the steps and tugged her into my lap. She was breathing hard, and her lips were slick and swollen.

"Here?" she asked, glancing to the door. There was no window in it, and no one had a key pass but the residents.

"Here. Gray and Emory went to the ranch."

That meant no one was going to interrupt us.

She met my gaze then stood, shucked off her shorts. I lifted up enough to push down my own, so my dick sprang free. "Shit. No condom." I glanced up the stairs as if I could wish one would magically appear from my room.

As she dropped her shorts to the concrete floor, she said, "I'm on the pill. I'm clean."

I had to grip my dick it ached so bad. "I've never gone bare before."

She set a hand on my shoulder to balance herself as she straddled me once more, keeping herself lifted, so I was at her entrance. She looked to me then lowered herself down. "Me either," she breathed as she worked her way onto me.

"Fuck," I breathed. She was hot and wet and tight and fucking perfect.

I never knew it could feel like this with nothing between us.

"Okay?" she asked me.

I frowned. "I've got my girl on my dick. I don't want to be anywhere fucking else."

I gripped her hips then lifted her up, pressed her back down. Then she took over, rocking and lifting, setting her sneaker-clad feet on the step to get leverage.

"Holy fuck, princess," I said, dying of pleasure.

I pushed up her t-shirt, and she lifted her arms long enough for me to toss it away. Then I worked her sports bra up over her tits, and I took one in my mouth. Her pussy clamped down, and she groaned.

We didn't last, this frantic fuck what we both needed. This wasn't what she'd have had with Larry. While this was straight up fucking, it was also a connection. She was right there with me. An even exchange. I was taking her bare. As she came all over me, coating me in her cream, I couldn't hold back and came deep inside her.

Making her mine. Fucking marking her. I was a Neanderthal, but I didn't give a shit. All I could do was say, "Mine."

25

Harper

"Stay by my side the entire time," Reed said. Again. "I hate this, Quake, just so you know. She shouldn't fucking be here."

We were in the parking lot of a vacant strip mall on the north side of Denver. Quake had called Reed this morning and told us about the meet up he'd arranged with Randy. We'd caught up with Quake and his son, Frankie, at the diner then followed them to this meeting spot.

"Noted," Quake replied, leaning against the hood of his SUV.

We weren't meeting for drinks. This wasn't some kind of work happy hour. This was how criminals got together. Although I didn't know enough about Quake to call him a criminal. Like he'd said, he had friends in low places. I couldn't judge him so harshly or at all when he was helping me. I couldn't understand what he got out of this, but I wasn't going to question.

I glanced around. The lot was deserted but public and on a busy street. No one was going to shoot each other—I hoped—in broad daylight with cars going by. I was still nervous and internally, I was freaking out. The guy we were waiting for had been the one to give me nightmares ever since he'd had his men try to kidnap me. I'd been trying to avoid him, and now I was intentionally going to face him.

Quake pushed off his SUV and came to stand beside me as a black Cadillac pulled in and parked. Randy got out along with two guys. Guys I immediately recognized.

I sucked in a breath and felt the adrenaline dump, remembering what they'd done.

The usually sunny Colorado sky had a layer of clouds that covered the sun. I shivered in my heavy puffy coat. With shaky fingers, I tucked my hat down lower on my head. Reed took my hand in his and gave it a squeeze. He was so warm. So calm. I had to wonder if he was afraid of anything.

"Those... those are the two," I whispered.

Quake stood on the other side of me. I was flanked by the president of an MC and a professional MMA fighter.

"Those two did what, doll?" Quake asked.

I couldn't tear my eyes away from those men. God. I saw them in my sleep. "From the hotel elevator two years ago."

"They're the ones?" Reed asked. This time, he squeezed my hand, and it wasn't for me. It was because he was pissed.

"Easy," Quake murmured. "Let's get through this meeting. Frankie will take care of them."

"With pleasure," he said, dark promise lacing the words.

I leaned around Quake to look at Frankie. He was around my age with dark curly hair and the palest blue eyes I'd ever seen. He had the lean, long legged physique of a runner. He was an inch or so shorter than his father, and the way he eyed Randy and his men, I assumed just as ruthless. He gave me a wink then put on the neutral mask that Quake and Reed both wore.

We stood in front of Reed's pickup and waited for them to approach. They stopped about ten feet away, and I felt like I was in a cowboy standoff.

"So, Harper Lane," Randy said. "We've been looking for you."

"Don't know why," Reed replied before I could even open my mouth. "She's got nothing to do with you."

All I could think of—besides freaking out—was that Randy had a Napoleon complex. He was shorter than me, his hairline receding probably at the same pace as his gut was growing. He was in his early forties, and he looked like the kind of guy who kicked puppies for fun.

"She's got something I want." His sleazy gaze raked over me, and I didn't miss the fact that he was talking about more than money.

I tugged on Reed's hand when I felt him coil up to strike. While he was good with his hands, he couldn't punch his way out of a gun fight.

"Easy," Quake murmured as Randy grinned, knowing his words had hit their target.

Reed gritted his teeth and said, "You want her brother."

"I want her money."

"I don't have it," I said.

He looked from Reed to me, pinned me with a stare as cold as the January weather.

"Your brother said you did."

"I figured you to be smarter than trusting a little shit like Cam Lane," Quake said, crossing his arms over his chest.

Even though it was hovering around freezing, he wasn't wearing a coat.

Randy's cheeks flushed with anger.

"She doesn't have the money," Quake repeated. "Cam's wrong."

I reached into my coat pocket, held up a folded piece of paper. "Here."

Reed grabbed my elbow thinking I was going to go over to Randy and hand it to him. As if.

I opened it, read the letter. "Dear Mr. Randolph," I began. I flicked my gaze up to Randy, then back to the email I'd received for my sizable donation in his name. "Thank you for your generous contribution. Your check for fifty thousand dollars will be a huge help in supporting the women and children of the community in receiving the support they need in leaving domestic violence or other unsafe family situations. You are a true hero in our community."

I stopped there, looked to Randy again. His fists were clenched tight. If looks could kill and all that. "You gave all that money away?"

"You did," I countered.

"Real nice of you to think of others," Reed said.

"A fucking hero," Quake added with a laugh, not the least bit concerned about Randy's anger.

Randy reached out, opened and closed his fingers. "Let me see that."

I handed it to Quake who moved to give it to Randy. The guy scanned the paper then crumpled it in his fist.

"That money has kept your brother alive. Cam Lane is now a dead man."

It was just as I'd thought. What I'd told the men at the

diner the other day. The best intimidation a guy like Randy had was threatening the life of a loved one.

I took a deep breath, let it out. Randy wasn't a threat to me any longer. And Cam? That was something else and not my problem.

"You think she gives a shit about her brother?" Reed asked. "He gave her to you. The fact she got away proves she's a better fighter than those two. You should be fucking glad I didn't pull them from their car in the gym's parking lot and finish them myself." Reed tipped his chin up indicating the guys from the elevator. They fidgeted on the pavement but didn't deny what they'd done or that they were a little afraid of Reed.

"She's under my protection," Quake told Randy, his words slow and clear. "If you or your men so much as look her way ever again, we're going to have problems."

Randy's beady eyes flicked over me then away.

"She's a fucking professor," Quake continued. "Not even in your league. Look at her man beside her. You think he's going to let this shit continue?"

Randy grunted. "I want your brother."

"We have to get him for you?" Reed asked.

"From what I hear, he's hiding out with Mommy and Daddy." Randy looked pointedly at me. "Might have to stop in and visit them all."

I couldn't help but laugh. Every one of them looked to me. "Mommy and Daddy like Cam a whole lot better than me. Tell them I said hi."

"Here's the deal, *Randy*," Reed began. "You leave Harper alone, and we'll let you keep your thumb up your ass where Cam's concerned. We'll give you a fucking trade when all I want to do is break your face."

Randy arched a brow but kept his mouth shut.

This was part of the plan. Me for Cam.

Reed turned me to face him and set his hands on my shoulders. I looked into his dark eyes and just... breathed. I was safe with him. With his touch, his heat seeping into me, I knew nothing was going to go wrong.

"Call him," he said, his voice gentle. For me. Only me. "Tell him you give up and will give him the money. The gym." He glanced at Randy. "Your guys know where it is since they've been camping out. I want to see that asshole taken away."

Randy didn't say a word.

I nodded, understanding what he wanted me to do. I pulled out my cell, swiped the number that I'd avoided for weeks.

"Jesus, Harper. Why the fuck haven't you called me? You're such a bitch." I pulled the cell away from my ear and hung up.

Reed's jaw was clenched tight having overheard. I took a deep breath. Called back.

"Hello, Harper." This time, he sounded much more pleasant. The way he could switch from angry asshole to smooth was another indication he was a psychopath.

"I give up. I'm..." I looked to Randy. "I'm scared. God, Cam, I can't even leave my building."

"Then give me the fucking money."

I sighed. "Fine."

"You always were useful for something," he replied.

"I can come now to your apartment." Clearly, he was desperate. The guy who'd made him that way was standing ten feet away from me.

"You want cash, I have to go to the bank," I told him.

"Fine. Two hours." He hung up.

I tucked my cell back in my coat.

"Good girl," Reed said then leaned down and kissed the top of my head. I exhaled and felt shaky. This was really happening. Cam was going to come to the building, and Randy was going to take him. Probably kill him.

"We're done here," Reed said to Randy, stepping back and pulling me with him. "He'll be at the gym in two hours. Give me fifteen minutes alone with him, and he's all yours. Then this shit is done."

"Yeah, yeah. If Cam shows, I won't even remember his sister's name." Randy looked from me to Quake.

They had a little stare down then Quake nodded.

Randy and his goons went to their car, and we watched them drive away.

"Hang in there, doll," Quake said, coming over and patting my shoulder. "It'll be over soon. You can stop running."

I looked to Reed, who nodded.

"I already have," I said to Quake but kept my gaze on Reed's. He pulled me into his arms, and I knew, even in a rundown strip mall, I was exactly where I wanted to be.

26

EED

I'D FOUGHT in the ring. Wanted to win. Always. After years of taking his shit, his belt and his hard-slung belligerence, I'd fought back against my dad. Had wanted him dead. Saw it done. Paid a big price for it.

But my father had been after me. His anger had been directed solely my way because I hadn't fallen in line. I might have gone along with his crimes, but I hadn't been in on them. I'd been able to handle it. Knew the score. Even knew I'd have to go to juvie to see him dead.

It had been worth every fucking minute of it.

But this Randy fucker? I'd wanted to stalk across the parking lot and finish him for even looking at Harper. He preyed on the innocent. Used them. Harper was strong and brave, but she didn't live in his world. Didn't know how low people went. How desperate. How dirty. Well, maybe she did with Cam, but he wasn't anything like Randy.

I wasn't sure if Cam was a sociopath or a psychopath. Maybe both, especially where Harper was concerned. But he was also a dumbass. He'd been born with a silver spoon in his mouth, taken the opportunities that afforded and made a good life for himself. Instead, he ended up owing a guy like Randy.

I knew what Cam would do for fifty K.

I knew what Randy would do for it.

Cam had offered his own fucking sister—again—to Randy, and he'd sent those two assholes after her. If she hadn't fought so hard, they'd have raped her then given her over to their boss. She'd have paid off Cam's debt that would have cost her so much more than a few zeroes on her bank balance.

She'd survived all the shit Cam had thrown at her. Again and again. She'd come out okay but taken a bunch of hits. The fight was over now. She had guys in her corner. Me. Gray. Quake, and since she was under his protection, the entire No Holds Barred crew. Thank fuck.

No matter how much I wanted to kill the asshole, Quake could take care of Randy, would ensure he forgot about Harper. But her brother?

Cam was going down, and I was going to see to it. Just like I had with my dad.

Only this time, I wasn't going to get my hands dirty. I was smarter now.

Randy knew there was no money. Cam was in big trouble. He'd pushed Randy off for two years—I was surprised Cam hadn't been shivved in prison—for Harper's cash. Randy was done waiting, and we'd hand the little shit over on a fucking silver platter.

We drove back to the building in silence. I'd held

Harper's hand in my lap, not letting go the entire way. Gray and Emory met us in the lobby.

"Sorry to pull you back from the ranch," I said to them.

Emory smiled at both of us, but Gray only nodded. He was in his usual non-workout uniform of jeans, snap shirt and Stetson.

"Gray filled me in on what's going on," Emory said, coming over and offering Harper a hug. Her hair was pulled back into a ponytail and concern filled her eyes as she glanced up at me over Harper's shoulder. She was a nurse practitioner and a mom, which made her like a mother hen, clucking around anyone who needed help, taking care of them. That was how we'd been connected with Quake Baker in the first place.

While Emory took care of everyone, Gray was the one who took care of her. *Nothing* would happen to Emory that was for fucking sure.

"Come up to our apartment. We'll get something to eat." Emory led Harper to the elevator, and I stood back with Gray.

"I shut the gym down early," he told me, tipping his voice low. "This gets messy, I don't want it happening in the parking lot."

"It's getting messy," I countered, cracking my knuckles.

Gray studied me for a moment then nodded. Over the summer, he'd gone off with Quake and Frankie to take care of the guy who'd broken into Emory's house. He'd never said what they'd done with him. I was smart enough not to ask. He knew how I felt, knew I wanted a few minutes with Cam. It wouldn't make things right, but it would sure feel fucking good.

The elevator doors slid open, and we went to join the women. Gray and Emory stepped into the car, and I looked to Harper. We'd only ever been on an elevator together that first time we met, the time she'd lost her shit.

"Stairs?" I asked. I'd skip the elevator whenever she wanted if that made her feel better.

She glanced at the elevator then me. "I'm good." Proving it, she took a deep breath and joined Gray and Emory, who held the button to keep the doors open.

Harper turned to face me and smiled.

That fucking smile.

I nodded then joined them.

I had no idea if she'd ever get on an elevator in other places, but here, she knew she was safe. It was a start. I'd take it.

Emory made some snacks while I stood with Harper by the window in Gray's and Emory's apartment. While there were two apartments on the second floor, mine and Harper's, there was only one on the third. It was open and spacious. Before Emory had moved in, the place was as neat as a fucking pin and minimal. Emory's things had added some life to the place. Plants, knickknacks and shit like that. It felt... homey.

Harper looked down into the parking lot. Waited.

I set one hand on the window ledge, the other on her hip and stood right behind her. I was trying to reassure her, but really, touching her made me feel better.

"You'll stay up here with Emory," I said. "No one can get up here. You'll be safe."

Again, the words were just as much for me as for her. I had to know while I was dealing with Cam that nothing was going to happen to her. I wasn't sure if Randy himself would show up to collect Cam or just Tweedldee and Tweedledum. Either way, I didn't want them anywhere near Harper while I was distracted beating the shit out of her brother.

She nodded. "I know."

I slid my hand down her back, felt the little bumps of her spine, then leaned in to murmur in her ear, so I wasn't overheard. "I want to take you to my shower. Wash away the filth of that meeting. You're too good to even do shit like that."

She shook her head, kept looking out the window. "No, I'm not. Not after all that Cam's done to me."

I spun her then to face me. Tipped her chin up with my fingers. "You survived, princess."

She rolled her eyes.

"You did," I repeated. "You think I'm the fighter? Fuck, woman. You've been fighting your whole life. It's over today. Done."

"I'll always be dirty," she whispered.

I slid my hand around to the back of her neck, cupped it. "Words like that piss me off. You into spankings, beautiful?"

Her eyes flared, and her mouth fell open. That cut the tension. While I'd had her a number of times, we hadn't gotten into anything kinky. I had no idea if getting her ass spanked got her hot. I'd never done it before, but if it was something she needed, I'd give it to her.

"You want to be with me any less because of my past?" I asked. "Because of my family?"

"No, of course not."

"Same goes for me. You were given a shitty family just like me. So we make a new family. You and me."

This time when her eyes widened, it was because of surprise. "What?"

I couldn't believe I had to spell it out to her. "I love you, Harper Lane."

Her eyes welled with tears.

I ran a hand over my head. "Fuck, the first time I tell a woman I love her, and I make her cry."

That made her laugh, and she wiped the tears away. "No. I'm not crying."

"I'm not all that smart, but I know tears when I see them."

"I'm not crying because I'm sad. I'm... I'm happy. I want to be your family too."

I exhaled and smiled. "Thank fuck."

"I love you, Reed Johnson," she said in the softest, sweetest, most perfect voice ever.

I kissed her then. Long and hard.

She loved me.

Me. The fuck up. The fighter. The guy so broken I figured I was unredeemable. The only place I could win was in the ring.

But with Harper, I won the championship title. I had no idea how I got so lucky.

I pulled back, leaned my forehead against hers.

"When Cam comes, I don't want you to get hurt."

I pulled back, stroked my hand over her hair. "I think you really are itching for a spanking. I get you in bed later, and your ass is going to have my handprint on it, yeah?"

"Reed."

"Don't insult me, princess. I can handle Cam. I need to know he's done. I need him to know that to get to you, he's got to get through me. Besides, payback's a bitch, and Randy's going to take care of his ass. After I'm finished with him."

A car door slammed, and we looked down into the lot.

When Harper stiffened beside me, I knew that was Cam. The fact that he climbed from a fancy Beemer made me wonder why he didn't fucking sell it to settle his debt or if he'd borrowed his Mommy's car.

We were too high up to get a good look at the guy, but he was here. I'd be close up soon enough.

Turning her to face me, I kissed her again, not lifting my head as I heard Gray approach.

"Stay here with Emory. After, I got plans for you, yeah?"

"Yeah."

$\mathcal{H}$ARPER

"WE CAN'T JUST SIT up here and eat hummus and crackers," I said, pointing at the plate of snacks Emory had sat on the counter. How she could calmly make something healthy to eat while my man—and hers—were downstairs having a *chat* with Cam was beyond me.

She turned from the fridge where she was filling a glass with ice, offered me a small smile. "Reed wants you safe. He cares for you."

I knew that. He'd said the L word. Him. Reed, the big, brawny fighter *loved* me. Butterflies filled my stomach like a thirteen-year-old girl having her first crush. Then it switched to dread. Panic.

"I need to know this is done," I replied, hugging myself. "I can't... I can't wonder if Cam's ever going to bother me again."

Emory cocked her head, offered me a small smile. "I have no idea what Gray did to that guy who broke into my house. Quake said I never had to worry about him again, but did that mean he'd been scared straight? In jail? Dead? I have no idea."

I stood on the far side of the counter beside the two bar stools, and she came across the kitchen to face me.

"Do you worry he'll come back?" I asked.

She shook her head. "No. Gray said I was safe, and I believe him. But I... I want to know what happened. Deep down, I still feel scared sometimes. Don't tell Gray, or he'll lose his mind."

Her words matched what I was feeling in my gut. I was done being scared. I loved the idea of Reed protecting me from Cam, but he couldn't protect me from my thoughts and fears, no matter what he told me going forward about being safe.

I had to know. I had to face Cam and stand up to him on my own. Looking him in the eye so he knew I couldn't be used anymore was important. Crucial. This was my only chance.

Spinning on my heel, I dashed toward the stairs. "I'm going down there. I need Cam to know he can't hurt me any longer."

I took the steps two at a time and didn't know Emory was following until I heard her footfall behind me.

We came out into the lobby, and I peeked through the glass doors into the gym. It was empty except for Reed, Gray and Cam.

Glancing at Emory, I took a deep breath and went through the doors.

"I told you, it's over," Reed said, his back to me, arms crossed over his chest. There was none of the usual music coming through the speakers, and his voice cut through the open space. "There is no money."

They were over by the fighting ring, Gray standing between Cam and the exterior door.

I hadn't seen Cam in two years. His hair was longer. He'd lost weight. He was angry, and there was an air of desperation around him. A wildness. "There's a shit ton of money. Harper needs to give it to me. Now."

"Not happening," Reed countered. His voice was deep and ruthless, completely different than how it sounded when he was with me.

"She owes me!" Cam shouted.

Emory tugged on my arm and pulled me behind the front desk. We had a clear view of the guys, but I had to assume she was intentionally putting the counter between us and Cam. Just in case. He'd have to get through Reed and Gray first.

"She owes you shit," Reed stated. "You gambled. You lost. You pay up on your own."

"I did."

"With your fucking sister."

A slow smile spread across his face. "No one fucked my sister. That's the problem. Randy still wants payment."

I didn't even see Reed raise his fist, but he'd slammed it into Cam's nose so fast I gasped.

"Fuck!" Cam shouted, bending down and covering his face with his hand. Blood poured around it, dripping down his chin and onto his shirt.

Reed and Grey turned their heads in our direction. Reed's eyes narrowed seeing me, and Gray didn't even blink although his eyes narrowed slightly when he glanced at Emory. Cam was too busy dealing with his nose to even notice. Reed grabbed Cam by his shirt and dragged him up the stairs and into the fighting ring, pretty much carrying him when he stumbled. The sides of the ring were metal fencing, the support poles covered with protective padding, just like I'd seen on the TV fights. Grey went up and pulled the access door closed behind them.

"Your sister gave the money to charity," Reed announced.

Cam stood up straight but kept his hand to his face. His eyes flared wide, not expecting that. "What the fuck?"

"You're on your own with Randy."

"What? No! She wouldn't do that."

"Yes, Cam. I would," I called.

Cam's eyes widened as he walked toward the fencing, curled his fingers around the wire. Gray stood at the top of the steps, blocking his exit. Unless he wanted to climb over the ring's walls, Cam wasn't getting out.

"You got that money because of me," he said.

I set my hands on the front desk's counter, leaned forward. "Hush money for what you did, *giving* me to Randy, just like you gave me to Brad when I was thirteen."

I felt Emory's hand settle on my shoulder, but she said nothing.

Cam smiled. "Brad. Fuck, I'd forgotten about that. As for *my* money, you wouldn't have gotten it if not for me,"

He was delusional.

"I've never wanted anything from you, Cam. As Reed said, the money's gone. I'm out. You need to leave me alone."

He laughed, his teeth bloody. "Leave you alone? You set these fuckers on me." He stuck an arm out and pointed at Reed.

I shook my head, but at the sound of the exterior door opening, I whipped around. Randy and his two guys came through the door, stopped just inside. For once, I was glad to see them. If anything, I had to give Randy credit for being prompt.

If I'd had even a glimmer of doubt about them taking Cam and doing... whatever to him, it was gone. I had no guilt. No conscience where he was concerned.

"I didn't set Reed and Gray on you," I said then pointed to Randy. "I set *your* goons on you."

"What?" Cam's eyes widened, for the first time out of fear. "No! Tell them you've got more money. That you'll give it to them."

"Get it from Mom and Dad," I replied. "They've bailed you out of everything else."

He shook his head, blood dripping onto the mat. "They won't. They can't. They're broke."

That surprised me, and my mind stalled. They had no money? The infamous Lanes, broke? That made no sense, but I was sure Cam was correct. He'd no doubt hit them up first thing he got out of jail. I wondered if my father was a gambler as well. Maybe bad investments. I didn't really care. I had a trust fund from my grandparents they couldn't touch. I had my job and didn't need fancy things like they did. Money didn't buy happiness, that was for sure.

"We done here?" Randy asked, clearly impatient.

"I'm done," I told him. I was. Cam was just as worthless as ever. He'd never change. I glanced at Emory and nodded. I didn't need to see anything else. I didn't need to watch as Randy took Cam away. I'd gotten what I'd come downstairs for. Closure.

We cut past Randy and went over to the doors to the lobby. I looked over my shoulder at Cam in the ring one last time then to Reed who stood beside him.

Reed's body was tense, his muscles primed and ready, just like during his past fights I'd watched online. I gave him the smallest of smiles, hoping he understood why I had to go against what he'd asked me to do and stay upstairs.

"Harper! No! Get your fucking ass back here!" Cam yelled.

I ignored him, only had eyes for Reed.

While Cam continued to yell at me, Reed winked.

Cam lunged for Reed, probably trying to catch him when he was distracted, but Reed hopped back and swung out, blocking Cam, then countering with an uppercut to the stomach that lifted Cam off the ground before he fell to the floor, wheezing.

Reed looked my way again, his jaw clenched this time, but he grinned at me. He was enjoying this. Yeah, we were good.

I pushed through the door then and cut across the lobby. Pushed the button for the elevator and heard Cam yelling again.

The elevator doors opened, and I stepped on, Emory following. I left Randy and those guys behind. Even though they were less than fifty feet away and I was getting on an elevator just as I had when the whole mess began, I knew now they couldn't touch me any longer. They were finally going after the right person. I was free.

"You good?" she asked, concern lacing her words.

As the doors slid closed, shutting out the last of Cam's shouting, I looked to her. Smiled.

Reed would come to me, and we'd live happily ever after, or whatever our version of it was. MMA matches and medieval cathedral visits.

"I'm good. I'm *so* good."

28

EED

"HARPER!" I shouted as I pounded on her door.

This time, she opened right away. I didn't say another word, just picked her up and kept on walking right to her bathroom.

"Reed, what—"

"Shh," I replied, setting her on her feet, so I could reach into her shower and turn on the water. I rinsed my hands off under the warming spray.

My adrenaline was flowing. I was amped just like after a fight in the ring. This one was different. I didn't have to go five rounds, and there had been no rules.

I'd won. Again.

This time, the prize was more than cash.

It was Harper's freedom.

Reaching behind my neck, I tugged off my t-shirt, used it to wipe my hands dry. I checked my knuckles and saw that the little bit of Cam's blood that had been on them was gone. Only then did I drop the shirt to the floor.

Harper eyed me, the look in those dark eyes a mixture of worry and heat.

"You don't have an ounce of fat on you," she said, her hand resting on my chest. While my dick got hard knowing she liked what she saw, I was surprised *that* was what she was thinking about right now.

I sucked in a breath, and I clenched my abs at the heat of her. Her fingertips were a fucking tease.

"You're wearing too many clothes," I told her, tugging at her shirt and getting it off. Her bra was next, then I dropped to my knees on the tile and got her jeans and panties off at the same time.

"Reed," she said again, this time a whisper as she set her hands on my shoulders for balance.

I looked up at her. Fuck, I needed this woman. I was filled with hatred for her brother, that fucker Randy. Those assholes of his who'd tried to hurt her...

I'd been so pissed.

I hadn't let my need for revenge make me lose focus. I'd used all my skill as a fighter to keep my head on straight, to remember what was important. Cam dead. Harper off of Randy's radar permanently. And if Quake did his thing, there'd be bullets in the back of Tweedledee's and Tweedledum's heads soon.

I hadn't needed him, but Gray had been there as backup. It was his gym. His reputation if anyone found out what was going on. The Outlaw didn't give a shit what anyone thought, especially if we were making things right. Settling a score that was over a decade old.

Everything led to this moment when she was finally free, and I needed to know she was whole. Safe.

Mine. No one else would touch her like this. Hear her. *Feel her.* I was suddenly frantic for her. "I need to make you come."

Hooking my hands around the backs of her thighs, I held her in place as I put my mouth on her pussy. She stepped wide for me, and I licked her slit, got her taste on my tongue then found her clit.

"Reed!"

I worked her without any teasing, needing to get her off. Now. I built her up fast, her cries bouncing off the walls of the bathroom, her fingers tugging on my hair.

Those actions made me even more focused on getting her off. I loved those sounds. Loved her taste. Her need. She came the second I slid a finger into her tight heat, her body tensing, then going soft. I held her upright as I stood then carried her into the shower.

She was soft and pliant as I washed her and relearned every inch of her body.

As I ran my soapy hands over her shoulders and down her arms, I spoke, finally calm enough to do so. "When I saw you downstairs, I almost lost my shit," I murmured.

Beneath my palms, I felt her stiffen. "I needed... closure."

I kissed the long line of her neck, licked up a droplet of water.

"I know," I breathed. "I understand. That's why your ass isn't pink."

She turned and looked up at me, her hair slicked back, her skin glistening with the hot water.

"Is he... it's over?" she asked. I felt ten feet tall knowing she trusted me to take care of it.

"Yeah. Randy took him." I never thought I'd ever have any kind of alliance with that asshole, but he'd stood back and waited while I beat the shit out of Cam, then I'd happily handed the loser off.

"Without a fight?" she asked, a little V forming in her brow.

"When I finished with Cam, he wasn't conscious. Made it easy for Randy."

A little gasp escaped her lips, and her dark gaze met mine.

"Easy, princess. I didn't kill him, no matter how much I wanted to. All my fighting was in the ring."

She studied me, nibbled at her lower lip. I couldn't help but kiss that plump flesh. When I was done, she said, "You kept your hands clean."

I lifted them, looked at my battered knuckles from years of punches. For the first time ever, I didn't see my past. As I cupped her face, I realized those hands could also be for good. They held Harper when she needed me to be strong. They touched her reverently when she needed to know how beautiful she was. They worked her to orgasm. They were for *good* now.

"I did. I won't risk us for anything. But Cam had to know what he did to you wouldn't go unpunished."

"Randy will see to it," she said.

When she blinked water from her eyes, I turned us, so she was pressed against the wall, and the spray was at my back.

"No. I don't know what Randy will do to him. Not our problem. But whatever he does, it's because of the shit Cam got into with him not what he did to you. Two years ago and when you were thirteen. If he survives—" I didn't think he was going to come out of this alive, but I wasn't going to tell her that. "—then he'll know not to get near you."

Her hands roamed over my body before she took my

dick into a snug grip. Stroked me from root to tip. "Fuck, princess."

"Thank you."

I took her wrist and tugged her hand from me. My dick wasn't happy, but that was too fucking bad. "Hang on. I don't want you thanking me through my dick, yeah? We're not going back to that shit."

Her eyes flared at my insinuation, and then she glanced away. Finally, she lifted her chin and looked up at me. Held my gaze. "I... I didn't mean it that way. Really. Thank you for helping me with Cam. With Randy. All of it."

"You're mine, and I—"

"Protect what's mine," she finished for me.

"I'll always take care of you," I promised.

She blinked, then gave me a small smile. "I know. You take good care of me." She took my dick in hand again. "Now can I *take care* of you?"

I reached blindly for the faucet and turned it off then tugged Harper out of the shower. Grabbing a towel, I dried her body, then tried to sop as much water from her hair before quickly drying myself.

"Bed. Now."

She turned and ran from the small room.

"You can run, princess," I called. "You can run faster than me. Farther, too. But I'll always catch you."

I stalked after her then, knowing my words were true. Harper was mine. I might be rough. But I was ready for her to be mine. Forever.

———

Thanks for reading Rough and Ready! It's time for more

hot cowboys in the Bachelor Auction series. Read Teach Me The Ropes!

Meet the Manning brothers in this steamy small town cowboy series from USA Today Bestselling author Vanessa Vale!

A bachelor auction. I was in a f-ing bachelor auction.
I wasn't a cow. A bull, definitely. When the ladies started to bid, it was looking rough.
Until she placed the winning bid.
The one I wanted. The woman who'd kneed me in the balls the other day.
Yeah, I was hot for a woman who wanted nothing to do with me. I was a guy obsessed.
She might be the teacher, but she was going to learn she was all mine and I wasn't letting her go.

If being a cowboy isn't enough, Sawyer's the town's fire chief. This book might burn up your ereader, but don't worry, he'll be there to put out the flames!

Read Teach Me The Ropes!

NOTE FROM VANESSA

Guess what? I've got some bonus content for you! Sign up for my mailing list. There will be special bonus content for some of my books, just for my subscribers. Signing up will let you hear about my next release as soon as it is out, too (and you get a free book...wow!)

As always...thanks for loving my books and the wild ride!

JOIN THE WAGON TRAIN!

If you're on Facebook, please join my closed group, the Wagon Train! Don't miss out on the giveaways and hot cowboys!

https://www.facebook.com/groups/vanessavalewagontrain/

GET A FREE BOOK!

Join my mailing list to be the first to know of new releases, free books, special prices and other author giveaways.

http://freeromanceread.com

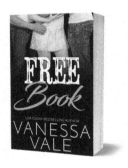

ALSO BY VANESSA VALE

For the most up-to-date listing of my books:

vanessavalebooks.com

All Vanessa Vale titles are available at Apple, Google, Kobo, Barnes & Noble, Amazon and other retailers worldwide.

ABOUT VANESSA VALE

Vanessa Vale is the *USA Today* bestselling author of sexy romance novels, including her popular Bridgewater historical series and hot contemporary romances. With over one million books sold, Vanessa writes about unapologetic bad boys who don't just fall in love, they fall hard. Her books are available worldwide in multiple languages in e-book, print, audio and even as an online game. When she's not writing, Vanessa savors the insanity of raising two boys and figuring out how many meals she can make with a pressure cooker. While she's not as skilled at social media as her kids, she loves to interact with readers.